The Fallen King

The Fallen King Chronicles Book 2

RICHARD FIERCE

CONTENTS

ACKNOWLEDGMENTS

This book wouldn't have been possible without my wife. She is always telling me, "Hurry up and write it so I can read it." I thank her for her persistent support and encouragement.

She's my rock.

—A beggar on the streets

CHAPTER 1

"You look ridiculous," Aramis scoffed.

Melchiades gasped in offense. "I will have you know that this is the current style in the court of your father." Aramis's attendant, and best friend, was constantly changing his wardrobe to mimic the nobles. "You look like a bird, Mel. Take that thing off."

Melchiades wore a medium-sized black hat with massive green plumed feathers that rose up from the back of the hat like some sort of sprouting plant. Mel shook his head indignantly and sputtered, which made him look even more like a giant peacock. Aramis burst into laughter and pointed to the door that led out of his personal quarters.

"I can't take you seriously. Now go and do something about your hat. I will meet you in the courtyard when I am ready." Mel sighed but did as he was ordered. When Mel had shut the door behind him, Aramis stripped his clothes off and tossed them onto the floor. The maidservants would gather them in the morning. They were muddy and smelled of sweat, the byproduct of his earlier escapades.

He stepped in front of the ornately decorated mirror that hung upon the wall next to his closet door and examined his reflection. His brown hair had lightened considerably in the last few weeks. His time outside with the soldiers must have had something to do with that. Stray hairs were beginning to grow along his jawline and chin. *I need to shave,* he thought.

He flexed his left arm, and then his right. They certainly looked larger. His abs didn't show, but he knew they would take longer to appear. A light yellow and green splotch the size of a fist mottled the skin below his right shoulder, just above his nipple. He gingerly touched it and winced at the pain. He had fallen from a horse and landed chest-first onto a rock.

It was a minor injury, but it was still sore. He hadn't bothered the court physicians with it, though his mother would be furious if she found out. He was the only son of the king, and she doted on him. He stepped into the closet and frowned. Mel had chosen something equally hideous for him to wear. "I don't think so," he muttered. Aramis grabbed a plain blue tunic and a pair of black pants. He liked simplicity, something that couldn't be said of Mel.

Melchiades was the son of a noble whose estate was on the edge of Oakvalor's eastern border. Some small house of nobility that he wasn't familiar with. He had arrived two years previous with instruction to serve the king in any way deemed appropriate. His father had plenty of servants, and so ordered Mel to attend his son.

Aramis had hated him at first. His ridiculous clothing, his odd accent, and his ardent faith in a god Aramis had never heard of. Over time, however, he began to respect the man. He was just as skilled, perhaps more so, than his father's finest soldiers and had a keen intelligence for matters of state. He didn't care for Mel's faith, but he admired his loyalty. Mel never skipped his private prayer time.

He slipped his freshly polished boots on and checked the mirror again. Nodding in satisfaction, he walked over to the window. His room was at the top of the keep and afforded him a magnificent view. Dusk was quickly approaching, and the lights of the city were beginning to burst forth into life. There was a ball tonight to celebrate his father's thirtieth year of reign, as well as Aramis's eighteenth year since birth.

Sadness welled up inside him as he thought about the day that should be joyous. His beautiful sister would not be present. The traitorous younger prince of Talvaard had murdered her, along with his own brother, before the two kingdoms could be sealed with peace by her marriage to the new king of Talvaard. His eyes filled with tears. He reached up and quickly wiped them away.

The sounds of the city below faintly reached his ears, pulling his mind away from the dark thoughts. He could barely make out the men returning from the mines. The smell of cooking fires and the meals they boasted made his mouth water. It reminded him of the roasted deer that was waiting at the ball.

He turned from the window and quickly left his room. Aramis didn't care much for the political nonsense that usually overshadowed his father's parties. The nobles were like a bunch of spoiled toddlers, whining and sniveling when they didn't get their way. And if there was one thing Aramis couldn't stomach, it was whining.

The hallway was a long corridor that stretched from the Royal Wing—where his father's chambers were—to the massive winding staircase known as the Circle that led down to the throne room. Aramis made his way toward the Circle. The walls of the hall were lavishly decorated, with giant richly colored tapestries and murals by famed artists throughout the land.

He passed a few guards who were stationed in the hall to keep curious guests from exploring the restricted areas of the castle. They stiffened at his approach and saluted as he passed. "Prince Aramis," they greeted formally.

Aramis nodded absently, thinking about the food that awaited him. He descended the Circle with measured steps, careful not to trip on the bright red runners that carpeted each stair. Despite the many servants who had toppled down the Circle, his father refused to have them removed.

He reached the bottom of the Circle and was greeted by Mel. "What are you wearing?" he demanded. "I picked out the best design for you to wear, and you come out wearing *that!*" Mel shook his head, which caused the feathers to sway back and forth.

Aramis smiled. "You know I don't like your taste in clothing if that's what you call it."

Mel feigned a look of anger and turned around as Aramis passed, escorting him out of the keep and into the courtyard. The sky had darkened considerably. A line of fire bowls glowed brightly, leading the way across the stone courtyard to the auxiliary building where his father always held his parties.

"It's going to be a smashing evening," Mel remarked enthusiastically. Aramis grunted in response. Mel gave him a sideways glance. "Did you invite Hanna to accompany you tonight?"

"Of course not," Aramis replied.

"Why not? I thought she rather enjoyed the royal parties?"

"Exactly. I don't want her to *expect* my invitations. I'm not sure where things between us are going, anyway."

"Your father likes her," Mel said with a grin.

"My father likes any pretty girl with money who shows an interest in his son. He has a legacy to think about."

"So, you wouldn't be terribly upset if she just happened to come of her own accord?" Mel asked, turning his gaze away from Aramis suspiciously.

"You didn't!"

"I would *never*," Mel breathed, aghast.

"Blast you, Mel. She won't leave me alone for weeks after tonight. Sometimes I don't know why I put up with you."

Mel laughed. "Please announce the prince," he instructed a servant who stood beside one of the fire bowls. The young man bowed and ran ahead of them. "Did you have to do that as well?"

"It's protocol," Mel answered.

"Now everyone will know I've arrived."

"That's the general idea."

Aramis sighed. "I hate the nobles."

"Hate is a strong word, don't you think?"

"Fine. I *dislike* the nobles. I won't put up with their petty complaints when I am king."

Mel didn't bother responding. Two large wooden doors were pushed open by several guards as they approached. Mel took the lead and entered first. A loud cheer rang out as Aramis entered. A wave of heat immediately hit him. With so many bodies in one place and no windows for ventilation, the heat was stifling.

Aramis spent the next hour talking to the many aristocrats who served in his father's court. It was completely un-enjoyable, but he suffered through it for the sake of his father's reputation. He couldn't care less what they thought about himself.

When he had finished exchanging pleasantries with the nobles, he made his way to the bar and began to partake of the various wines and liquors, mixing them with abandon. Aramis was vaguely aware of his father retiring from the party, not unusual for him. He might be healthy for his age, but he was no longer a young man.

Mel was participating in some new popular dance with several people, all wearing similar ridiculous looking hats. He would never understand 'fashion'.

"There you are," Hanna's familiar voice sounded beside him. He downed another cup of whatever he was drinking and turned to face her.

She was beautiful. Her long hair was a light blonde color and reached past the middle of her back. Her eyes were a brilliant blue, the bluest he had ever seen. That was one of the things that initially attracted him to her.

"Hannah," he said, smiling dumbly. Something in the back of his mind told him to keep his mouth shut, but he didn't listen. "I was hoping you'd be here."

No, I wasn't.

She gave him an enormous smile. His heart began to beat quickly. Inhibitions were all but gone, it seemed. She leaned in close to him and whispered, "I have a gift for you in honor of your life celebration."

"If it includes you, I can't wait to have it."

Why did I say that?

She blushed and shook her head. She held up a small wooden box. He hadn't even noticed she had anything in her hand. He accepted it from her and fumbled clumsily with it before opening the thing. Inside was a silver pendant inscribed with his family's crest: an oak tree with three branches. They represented the ideals his family strived for. Courage, honor, and justice.

"Thank you," he breathed. "It's beautiful. Like you." He allowed her to clasp it around his neck, then he ran the fingers of his right hand through her hair. Her smell was more intoxicating than any alcohol he'd ever tasted.

"My Prince," Mel interrupted. "It's time to retire for

the evening."

Aramis sighed. Mel was a blessing to him, as well as a curse. "You're interrupting Hanna," Aramis informed him. He turned his attention to his friend and winked. "You should retire without me," he whispered. Or at least he thought he whispered. Everyone nearby could hear him.

"It's quite all right," Hanna interjected. "I'll see you later." Aramis wasn't sure if she was stating a fact or asking a question. She curtsied and took her leave. "You're a killjoy sometimes, you know that?"

Mel grinned in reply. "I'm protecting you from yourself. Someone has to when you fill yourself with this stuff. Did you eat anything?"

Aramis shook his head. He had forgotten about food with all the nobles buzzing around him. Mel disappeared through the crowd of people and returned a few minutes later with a plate full of venison. "Eat this and then you can retire from the festivities."

Aramis grabbed a piece of the meat and stuffed it into his mouth. "The night has hardly begun. Why would I retire now?" he asked.

"I knew you would forget," Mel said. "You told your father you would go on the hunt with him tomorrow. And the night is later than you realize. It's after midnight."

Aramis cursed under his breath. "I did forget. Blast it, Mel! I hate going on those boring hunts. Sitting around for hours, listening to old men recount exaggerated tales of their 'glory days'. I prefer a *real* opponent. One who thinks and reacts. Not an animal that walks into a trap."

"I can imagine," Mel replied. Aramis cleared the plate and drank another cup of wine. "I think I will retire now."

Mel escorted him through the throng of people and to the doors they entered through earlier. Just as before, several guards pushed the doors open and saluted the prince. Mel thanked them for their service and led Aramis along the lighted path back to the keep.

"Should I assist you to your chambers?" he asked. Aramis waved his hand dismissively. "I'm not needy like my father," he answered. "I'll see you in the morning. And for mercy's sake, wear something practical tomorrow."

Mel bowed low in response.

Aramis left him behind as he entered the keep and ascended the Circle. The guards he'd passed earlier were no longer present. His father had probably released them earlier. He meandered along the hallway, humming an old song his mother used to sing to him.

Reaching his room, he paused and briefly considered going back down to the party. Perhaps Hanna would still be there …

He decided not to. It would be hard enough to get up already. Aramis entered his room. He kicked off his boots, neither landing near the other. He pulled his tunic over his head and tossed it to the floor.

Something glinted in the mirror as he passed it. He stopped to look and realized it was the pendant around his neck. He had already forgotten Hanna had given it to him. He admired it in the mirror. She was a clever one. Now he had to give her a gift, which would be seen as a move of official courting.

"I have no idea what I should get her," he muttered. He walked over to his window and opened it, letting the cool breeze in. Maybe it was the alcohol, but he was burning up.

He spied his father's window. Light shone from the room and he could see his father's servants fawning over him and preparing him for bed. If he could hardly stand Mel doing it for him now, what would it be like when he became king?

Aramis pushed the thoughts from his mind. His father was healthy and strong, unlikely to pass the crown down anytime soon. And that didn't bother Aramis one bit.

He was about to turn and climb into bed when he noticed something unusual from the corner of his eye. Leaning forward, he squinted and tried to see better. It looked like a shadow. It hovered in one spot for a moment, then shifted upward. It was almost like a pattern. Hover, shift.

"What is that?" he whispered to himself. As though fate had timed it perfectly, the moon illuminated the shadow for just a moment. It was a man. Yet why would a man be scaling the side of the …

Assassin!

Aramis turned and dashed across his room. As fear swept through him, he began to sober up. He threw the door open and dashed past a few startled servants. He sprinted through the hallway, his heavy footsteps muffled by the thick rugs that lined the floor. He glanced down every side passage, looking for guards. He didn't see any.

"Guards!" he shouted, "Guards! To the King's chambers!" He had no idea if anyone heard him. He ran faster, his legs burning from the effort. Two massive wooden doors separated the Royal Wing from the rest of the keep. Normally there were two guards positioned here, but he saw no one. What was going on? The doors were heavy, but he threw himself bodily into one, sending lances of pain through his bruised chest.

The door swung open slowly, just enough for him to squeeze through. And then he was running through the Royal Wing, his breath coming in ragged gasps. Was it possible the assassin had made it into his father's room yet? He didn't know. A lone soldier stood guard beside his father's door. Aramis almost slammed into him before stopping his momentum.

"Where … are the … others?" Aramis demanded, sucking precious air into his lungs.

"My lord?"

"Get … reinforcements! Hurry!"

The guard seemed confused. Aramis grabbed the soldier's sword and shoved him out of the way. "Do as I command! Get reinforcements!"

The guard bowed hastily and ran off down the corridor. Aramis kicked the door twice before it opened, splintering the wood and breaking the latch mechanism. He strode into the room to find his father—and the servants—staring at him in surprise.

"What is the meaning of this, Aramis?" the king demanded.

"Father! Step away from the window!"

"Have you gone mad, boy? What are you doing?"

Aramis rushed to the window and looked down. He didn't see anything or anyone. He pulled the window closed and locked it. "Father, I saw a man climbing the wall. He was clothed in black. It was an assassin, I'm sure of it. Did anyone come in through the window?" he asked the servants. They were looking at him as if he were crazy, but they all shook their heads.

Perhaps he had made it in time.

"A man climbing the … impossible! Aramis, what's going on? Are you drunk? Where are your cloth—?" Aramis cut him off mid-sentence. "I'm telling you, I saw someone from my window climbing the keep. Where are your guards?"

"What are you talking about? They are outside."

"There was only one soldier out there." Aramis's mind was racing. "I think you are in danger. We should go."

"In danger of who? We are not at war."

Aramis went to the door and peered down the hallway. *Where are they?*

"I beg to differ," an unfamiliar voice said. Aramis spun about and saw a strange man among the servants. His father kept only female attendants. The man brandished a dagger. "Kings always have enemies."

"Drop it," Aramis warned. He held the sword up before him and slowly advanced toward the man. The servants squealed in terror and scrambled to get out of the way.

"Why would I do that?" the man replied. "That just wouldn't be fair." The assassin rushed the king. Aramis threw himself into a roll and came up onto his feet in front of his father, deflecting the man's dagger with his sword. He launched a series of furious thrusts at the man, all of which the assassin managed to avoid. He could hear a commotion in the hallway and was relieved to know the guards were coming.

"You've failed," Aramis said triumphantly. "The guards will be here in a moment and you will be hanged at once."

The assassin flashed a smile at him. "That may be." Then the man rushed him. Aramis swung the sword as fast as he could, but he couldn't match the assassin's speed. He received several nicks along his left arm. The servants fled out into the hall, screaming as they ran.

Just a few more moments.

The assassin attempted to slide past his left, but Aramis stopped the man with an awkward swing of his sword. Seeming to anticipate the move, the assassin halted his momentum and pivoted, using Aramis's body as leverage to propel himself past the prince's right.

Aramis turned too late to catch the man, and the man lunged at the king with the dagger, trying to land a killing blow. His father was no novice to battle, however. He ducked down and grabbed the assassin's wrist, twisting it and jabbing the man's elbow with his palm. The dagger clanged harmlessly to the floor.

"Who sent you?" the king inquired angrily.

The assassin smiled again. "Wouldn't you like to know, *Your Majesty?*" The man used the title sarcastically. Aramis could hear the rattle of the soldiers' armor.

Any moment.

He held the sword out and pressed the tip of the blade against the man's side. "If you move, I'll gut you," he promised. "Answer my father's question. Who sent you?"

"It should be obvious," the man responded, "You know him."

The assassin deftly slipped his hand out of the king's grasp and slapped the flat of the sword blade hard, jerking the hilt out of Aramis's hand. In a fluid movement more graceful than anything Aramis had ever seen, the assassin grabbed the sword and drove it into the king's chest. Blood spurt forth and the king cried out in agony.

Aramis's eyes widened in horror and he lunged for the assassin. The man stepped out of his reach and landed a solid blow to his jaw. Aramis staggered back from the force and tried to maintain his balance. The assassin retrieved the dagger from the floor.

"Now your hell begins," the man said. The assassin pointed to Aramis's left arm and muttered something in a strange language. An intense burning flared through his arm. And then the assassin's cape fell to the floor and the man was gone.

Aramis didn't believe his eyes. Did the man *disappear?* He rushed to his father's side and grabbed the hilt of the blade. "Don't die, father. We'll get you to the healers. I promise!"

A contingent of guards entered the room. "He's killed the king," one of them shouted, "Seize him!" Confusion swept over Aramis like a cold ocean wave.

I didn't kill him! His mouth wouldn't work.

The soldier who he'd ordered to get help walked up to him and shook his head. "You killed him with my sword?" The soldier kicked him in the face. He collapsed onto the floor and there was only darkness.

"One decision does not define a man. Though it certainly changes him."

—Prince Aramis

CHAPTER 2

Aramis opened his eyes.

His head was throbbing. His mouth was dry, as well as his throat. The revelry from the night before, most likely. He tried to sit up but found his wrists bound at his sides by manacles.

"What the …?" the words were barely more than a whimper. His head rolled to the left. It was dark. Mostly. As his eyes adjusted to the gloom, he noticed a dim light flittering at the edge of his vision. His right eye felt swollen and he couldn't see clearly out of it. He surveyed his surroundings. Stone walls and a metal gate.

Where am I?

Aramis tried to jerk his arm free, resulting in pain shooting through his wrist. His hand was wet and sticky with something, but he wasn't sure what. He forced himself to calm down and breath. That was probably the only thing that didn't cause him pain.

His thoughts were groggy. He remembered the ball.

The nobles, Mel's outlandish dancing. He also remembered drinking. How could he forget that? Going back to his room, though, that was merely fuzziness. The cool air of the strange room brought his attention to the fact that he wasn't wearing a shirt.

I remember talking it off ... I looked out the window ... the window!

The memory washed over him, overwhelming him with the horrifying knowledge that his father was dead. The tears stung his swollen eye, but he couldn't hold them back. He sobbed for long moments before regaining control of his emotions.

The man who had killed his father would pay. He would send the armies out to hunt the assassin down. Aramis vowed to himself that he would personally kill the man responsible.

With his father dead, that meant that he was now the king. A terrible weight settled over him. He knew one day the throne would be his responsibility, but not now. Not like this. He thought he could hear voices. They spoke quietly, and he couldn't make out their words.

Aramis continued staring in the direction of the light, trying to determine where he was. He had no idea whether it was morning or night. He didn't recognize anything. The sound of jingling keys startled him. The metal gate swung open and an indistinct form stepped inside.

"You're awake," an unfamiliar voice said. The tone was gruff and reminded him of the soldiers he spent his days with. "It's about time. He must have roughed you up good."

"Who?" Aramis tried to say, but his throat was too dry and constricted to manage more than a mumble. A fit of coughing overwhelmed him. "Save your energy," the man bade him. "You'll need it. You can believe that."

There was something about the way the man said those words that unsettled him. What did he mean? The man came close and knelt down beside him. Aramis couldn't make out the man's features in the darkness. The man was fidgeting with something.

"The blasted thing is stuck," he muttered to himself. An earsplitting screech caused Aramis to flinch. The bed he was manacled to begun to rise.

After a minute or so, he was completely vertical. Were it not for his bindings, he felt as though he would have fallen onto the floor. At the bottom of the bed, where his feet were, was a thin metal lip that rose off the bed. His feet rested on it, which kept them from dragging on the floor.

Then he was rolling toward the gate. The bed had wheels. That was interesting. The man rolled him out of the room and into a short narrow hallway. He could see now the light that had caught his eye before was only a torch on the wall, one of a few that were spaced irregularly along the hall. He was wheeled down the hall and to the left, into a similar room. This one had an open doorway; no gate.

A brazier filled with burning coals gave the room a reddish hue. The man left him facing the glow of the brazier. Aramis didn't mind at all. It felt good. He hadn't realized before, but he was shivering. The warmth was a welcome indeed.

"Sit tight," the man said. "He'll be along shortly."

Aramis considered responding but decided not to waste his breath. The man probably wouldn't answer anyway. He gazed at the glittering coals for what felt like hours, though how much time had truly passed he couldn't guess. Time ceased to have meaning in the darkness. The sound of heavy footsteps echoing through the hall broke his reverie.

"Lord Aramis."

The use of his name gave him pause. Wherever he was, this man recognized him. The new person came around and stood in front of Aramis. The angles of his face were sharp and defined. His hair was black; his eyes light gray. He stood as tall as Aramis, though the prince was at least a foot off the ground in his wheeled bed.

The man offered a slight bow. He seemed to analyze Aramis with a critical eye for a moment, then turned to one of two tables that stood to each side of the brazier. A silver carafe and a wooden cup were the only adornments. The other table was covered with a white cloth. The man lifted the carafe and poured a liquid into the cup.

He exchanged the carafe for the cup, then turned back to Aramis. He lifted the cup to Aramis's lips, but Aramis refused to open his mouth. It was probably poison. "It's water," the man said as if reading his mind. "Drink."

Aramis hesitated, then allowed his lips to part far enough for the man to pour the liquid into his mouth. The water was cool and refreshing, soothing his dry throat. He could feel the water run down his esophagus and into his stomach. It was an odd feeling. He drank the entire cup. "More?" the man asked.

Aramis shook his head. "Where am I?" he asked softly.

"You are in the keep. The dungeon, specifically."

The dungeon? "Why?"

The man seemed surprised at the question. "For murdering your father—the King—of course."

"I didn't …" Aramis sighed. "I didn't kill my father. Why would I?"

"I was hoping you would tell *me* that," the man answered. "There are several witnesses who say they came upon the scene. You had your hand on the weapon. A sword you took from one of your father's guards, I believe. Do you deny it?"

"I deny killing my father, yes. If I had my hand on the sword, I don't remember. There was a man who scaled the wall of the keep. *He* killed my father."

The man folded his arms across his chest. "You expect me to believe a man climbed the walls of the castle? That's a task I would say is impossible. And your father's wizards have warded the entire castle against magic."

"I thought the same. But it happened. I saw it with my own eyes. I ran to my father's room to warn him, but the assassin had already entered through the window when I arrived." His throat was constricting. "May I have some more water?"

The man nodded and refilled the cup. Aramis downed it all. The water intensified his feeling of hunger. "Suppose someone was able to do as you say. Where then did he go?"

"After he stabbed my father, I tried to attack him. He eluded me and then … then he disappeared. I don't understand it myself," he said, seeing the doubt evident on the man's face.

"There are two types of people in this world," the man said. "Those who hide the truth, and those who reveal it. I am of the latter of the two. My name is Jarn, and I have a long list of truths I have revealed. The tale you have crafted is a clever one, I will grant you that. But I will get the truth out of you, one way or another."

"That is the truth," Aramis protested. "Why would I lie about it?"

"Men lie for various reasons. I believe you wanted the throne. Your father was healthy, and you were impatient. Hence, you murdered him."

"I did not kill my father." Tears welled up in his eyes. The man spoke so nonchalantly about the death of his father, as though he couldn't see how torn up Aramis was about it. He loved his father more than anything.

Jarn pulled a ring of keys from his belt. He fingered through them until he found the one he was searching for, then unlocked the shackle that held Aramis's left arm. Aramis groaned in relief.

Jarn walked over to the table that was covered with the cloth, grabbed the edge, and pulled it over beside Aramis's bed. He placed Aramis's hand onto the table and cuffed it into place with a metal shackle attached to the table.

"I almost believe you," Jarn said. Turning to the brazier, he retrieved a pair of tongs from a hook set in the wall. Using the utensil, he dug through the coals and withdrew one.

"Almost," he said. And then he promptly placed the coal on the back of Aramis's hand.

Aramis sucked in his breath, then let out a shriek of pain. The coal burned his flesh, a searing intense sting. It was all he could do to say, "Stop!"

Jarn waited a few seconds more before removing the coal and placing it back in the brazier. "That was quick. I have found that pain usually helps one to remember the truth--."

Aramis grit his teeth against the pain. "I, I … didn't …"

Jarn frowned. "A pity. I thought you would come clean quickly. No matter. I have several ways to get what I want." He placed the tongs back onto the wall hook, then removed the cloth from the table. An array of various wicked looking tools and a few vials greeted him.

He picked up a small hammer and an odd-looking tool that resembled the tongs, but smaller. "Water eases the pain of burns as I'm sure you are aware. Would you like me to pour some onto your hand?"

Aramis remained silent. Jarn nodded as if expecting

as much. "These are forceps. You may not be familiar with them, but you will be well acquainted shortly." Jarn angled the forceps so that the prongs were horizontal. He placed the nail of Aramis's index finger between the edges of the forceps.

"Some like to heat the prongs up until they are red hot," Jarn said. "I prefer not to. Brace yourself. This is really going to hurt." In one fluid motion, Jarn clamped the prongs down and yanked his arm backward.

Aramis screamed again as his nail was ripped off. Blood welled up from his nail bed. The pain was agonizing. He got lightheaded and thought he might lose consciousness. "That is only half of the procedure," he vaguely heard Jarn say. "This is the second half."

He watched his torturer raise the hammer. Everything appeared to be moving in slow motion. The hammer descended, smacking directly in the middle of his finger. Aramis both heard and felt the bone crack beneath the blow. The pain was too much for him to bear. He could feel the darkness closing in. He invited it to take him.

In the distance, he heard Jarn's voice, "Not so fast." A sharp smell in his nostrils brought his senses reeling back. Jarn was waving one of the vials from the table under his nose. "I cannot do my duty if you aren't feeling the effects of my methods. We have only just begun. And you will not pass out. I will not allow it."

The next twenty minutes were the longest and most brutal Aramis had ever experienced. Jarn proceeded to tear the nails from the remaining four fingers, breaking the bones afterward with the hammer. And each time Aramis thought he might find relief from the pain in the darkness that threatened his vision, Jarn would wave the vial under his nose.

Finally, when Jarn broke the last finger of his left hand, he questioned Aramis further. When Aramis held to the fact that he had not killed his father, Jarn got frustrated and left the room.

Aramis was weak. His muscles shuddered involuntarily. His battered fingers were numb and useless. His eyes had ceased to produce tears. His mind was deadened by grief and pain.

I'm going to die.

The realization didn't scare him. It was more of a psychological surrender to the fact that his life was at an end. Jarn seemed passionate enough that he would end up killing him trying to get a confession. And Aramis refused to lie about doing it for the sake of respite. To do so would dishonor his father's memory.

His eyes took in the carnage of his mutilated hand. He noticed something else. A faint black mark on his forearm. Perhaps it was a trick of the light, or merely a bruise, but there was a shadowy symbol in his flesh.

Strange.

Then his vision blurred and he closed his eyes to keep from being sick.

● ∞ ● ∞ ●

"Aramis! Lord Aramis!"

Aramis cracked his eyes open slowly. He awoke to find his attendant Melchiades staring at him. "Mel?" he croaked. His hand was still numb, and his entire body was aching.

"Praise Edria! I thought you were dead. Don't move," Mel warned. He struggled with the shackles that kept Aramis bound to the bed. He growled in frustration. Aramis watched through blurred eyes as Mel searched the table covered with torture instruments.

Grabbing something thin, he slid it into the keyhole and jerked it back and forth viciously. He issued a laugh of triumph as the manacle made a click and popped open. He did the same to the other one. As soon as his bonds were released, Aramis fell forward weakly.

Mel quickly grabbed him to keep him from crashing onto the floor. "I fear I must ask you a foolish question, my Prince. Are you able to walk?"

Aramis shrugged weakly. "Water," he whispered, nodding toward the table with the carafe. Mel hesitated, then grabbed it and helped Aramis drink.

"I don't mean to be inconsiderate to your pains, but we must make haste. The guards will be back at any moment."

Aramis lay in silence, forcing his body to obey his will. He could sense an urgency in Mel's voice and trusted his friend enough to know there was a good reason behind it. He drank some more water. "Help me up."

Mel complied, pulling Aramis by his arms and onto his feet. He was able to stand up without help, but he didn't know if he would be able to walk on his own. He tried to take a step and almost collapsed.

"Here," Mel said and wrapped Aramis's arm around the back of his neck. "Lean on me. It will slow us down, but we don't have any other options." Aramis didn't say anything, choosing instead to conserve his energy. They walked out of the room and into the hallway. "I don't know where we are," Aramis admitted.

"No worries, my Lord. I know this place well." Mel motioned to the right. "That leads to a stairwell that takes you up into the main keep. This way," he pointed to the left, "is the way we are going. There is a hidden tunnel that will take us out by the river."

Aramis didn't know what was happening, other than the fact that Jarn assumed he was guilty of murdering his father. "What is going on, Mel? I'm so confused."

"Come, I'll explain as we walk. We must hurry." Leaning most of his weight onto his friend, Aramis followed Mel's lead. The corridor seemed to be fairly straight, other than a few passages that broke off to the sides.

"The king has been killed," Mel said tentatively. Aramis nodded silently. "Rumor among the court is that you are responsible for the act. Some believe it, others do not. Fortunately, none of the nobles are squabbling for power."

That surprised Aramis immensely. He figured without his presence to hold the kingdom together, there would be much infighting.

"The people know you are being detained, but I highly doubt they know you are being tortured down here. There would be rioting in the streets. Jarn is a seriously disturbed individual." Mel paused and cocked his head. "They're coming." He quickened his pace and Aramis struggled to keep up.

"Forgive me, my Prince." Mel shook his head despondently. "I should have escorted you to your chambers that night. I failed in my duty."

"It's not your fault," Aramis replied weakly. "You didn't know what would happen. No one could have known what last night held."

"Last night? You've been gone three days."

Aramis's surprise was broken by the sound of guards shouting. "They know," Mel said. "Quickly!" They tried to pick up their pace, but Aramis was too exhausted.

They continued down the hall until it ended in a cul-de-sac. The walls were smooth, marred only by several torches. For a dead end, the area was well lit. "Are we going the wrong way?" Aramis asked tiredly. Mel shook his head. "The entrance to the tunnel is hidden. There should be a stone or something out of place. That is the trigger to open the door."

Aramis leaned against the wall as Mel searched for it. He could hear the voices of their pursuers closing in. Five armed and heavily armored guards came around the corner.

"Halt!" One of the guards stepped forward from the others and drew his sword. The other four also unsheathed theirs. "By order of the King, you are hereby detained for the unlawful release of a prisoner."

Mel turned to face the soldiers. "The King has been murdered, you inconsiderate fools! This man is Prince Aramis, now King Aramis. Show some respect."

"I know who he is," the leader of the group said, staring at Aramis. "We've been ordered to execute him." The soldier turned his attention to Mel. "As well as anyone aiding him."

"I wouldn't do anything hasty if I were you," Mel said. Aramis looked at him. There was something about his friend that seemed different.

"Surrender willingly and your death will be painless," the soldier promised. A large smirk spread across Mel's face.

"Take him," the leader ordered, pointing his sword in Aramis's direction. Aramis tried to move away from them, but his legs gave out and he collapsed face first. The two guards moved in to grab him.

Mel leaped forward suddenly, landing in front of the prince and shielding him with his body. Aramis rolled onto his back. What he watched unfold was like something out of a dream.

The air around Mel shimmered with mist. The torches darkened momentarily, flaring erratically. The mist began to coalesce around Mel's body, shifting and transforming into armor.

Silver and flawless, the armor was similar to plate mail Aramis had seen before but unique in a way he could not explain. The soldiers hesitated, unsure of what to do. Mel held his hand out and a sword formed, the same color and style as his armor.

One of the guards turned and fled, obviously wanting

no part in the fight. The leader looked from Mel to Aramis, then back to Mel. He rushed forward, swinging his sword in an arcing motion. Mel easily stepped out of his reach, moving much faster in plate armor than any soldier Aramis had seen before.

As the soldier's momentum took him forward, Mel thrust his own blade out, striking the soldier in the thigh. His sword pierced straight through the soldier's armor, his leg, and through the back of the armor.

The man gargled in pain, dropping to a knee. Mel withdrew the blade and turned to the other three soldiers, who thought to rush him. Mel gripped the hilt in both hands and held the sword up before him. A dazzling light blinded the guards. They staggered forward, trying to shield their eyes from the glow.

One of the soldiers reached out toward the light. He screamed as his hand was instantly incinerated. Turning, he also fled. The other two dropped their weapons and knelt before Mel. "I surrender!" one of them said.

"As do I," the other chimed in. Mel lowered his sword and the light faded, leaving the hall darker than before.

"Take your captain and retreat." The soldiers rushed to their feet and over to the man clutching his leg. They dragged him by the arms and took flight down the corridor. Mel returned to the wall and after a moment of searching pushed on a stone that was barely sticking out from the others. The floor shook as the wall trembled visibly and then slid into a hidden panel.

Then he lifted the prince effortlessly off the floor and over his shoulder and entered the tunnel. Aramis's mind was reeling. What did he just witness? He looked around and noticed the walls were not made of stone like the dungeon but were carved directly into the dirt. Everything was pitch black except for Mel's armor.

It radiated a faint luminescence. In the middle of the

back plate, right below Mel's neck, was a symbol etched into the armor. A closed hand with an eye in the middle of it. It didn't strike any chords with Aramis; he'd never seen it before.

After roughly a hundred yards, the tunnel ended, and they were walking in the open landscape surrounding the castle walls. It took a moment for his eyes to adjust to the brightness. The sun was nearing the middle of the sky. Just as Mel had said, the Stalwart River flowed nearby.

Mel walked over to a small copse of willow trees on the bank of the river and set Aramis on the ground. The air shimmered briefly, and then Mel's armor was gone. The two stared out at the river in silence. Aramis looked at the man he had been friends with for two years, still trying to comprehend everything.

"How did you do that?"

"The question isn't who is going to let me. It's who is going to stop me."

—Jovanna

CHAPTER 3

She smelled the smoke before she saw it.

The pungent stench that assaults the nostrils and clings to your clothes long after the smoke is gone. Jovanna stepped out of her stone and mud house and looked around to glimpse what was burning. Nothing she could see.

Tiny gray flakes of snow began to fall. She held out her hand to let some of the flakes collect in her palm. They were warm.

Her eyebrows rose in curiosity. Snow wasn't warm. She ran her index finger through the flakes and they smeared across her skin. It wasn't snow.

It was ash.

Jovanna looked to the edge of the village and noticed a crowd had gathered. Deciding to see what was happening, she walked down the dirt path that wended its way through the small village. The place felt deserted. She was used to large cities so densely packed with people that it was hard to walk without bumping into others.

She welcomed the change and the solitude, as she didn't really care for people. As she reached the edge of the village where the people had gathered, she could see massive clouds of smoke in the distance. She avoided the multitude and stood off to the side by herself.

She could hear the people murmuring, but she didn't bother to listen. They could be a superstitious lot. She scanned the horizon and saw the black clouds were billowing up from beyond the border of Talvaard.

"The fires of war," his voice startled her, though she did well to hide it. Jovanna looked at him and shrugged.

"Talvaard is without a king, and many are trying to take the throne by force. Several of the generals are using their armies to their own advantage."

"Jerik, I don't know why you bother my ears with your petty trifles. You know I don't care." She turned from him and began walking back toward the village.

"If you don't care," he called out to her, "then why are you still here?"

Jovanna ignored him and continued walking. She found his constant barrage of information annoying. The old man acted like he knew everything. The ash was falling thicker now. The war for the throne was none of her concern. This village was located in the Deadlands, not Talvaard, and she found it highly doubtful that the battle would go beyond Talvaard's border.

Jerik had saved her life, true. In her reckless attempt to use the dragon's sphere to gain power, she had frayed the magic. The result had been a potent explosion that had almost killed her.

Jerik was an enigma to her. He was old, ancient even. He led the Guardians, an unknown band of people who worked unseen to keep the balance in the world. He had used his power to save her and brought her to this remote village where he lived among the elven tribes of the Deadlands.

Jovanna spotted Velent, the chieftain's son, returning from a hunt. He didn't look happy. He stepped wide of her as he passed by, an elven form of snubbing someone.

"Careful," she said loudly. "You wouldn't want to offend the wrong person." He stopped mid-stride and puffed his chest out defiantly, glaring at her. She returned his gaze with equal ferocity. She rested her hand on the hilt of her sword, tapping her finger on the pommel.

He looked like the rest of the elves she had seen. Lithe and tall, with long brown hair and black eyes. His arms were covered in tattoos. They weren't for decoration, Jovanna knew. They were weapons, every one of them. From the time an elf could walk, they were tattooed with magical symbols and taught how to use them.

She enjoyed toying with him. He was too honorable to fight her, but he was open about his hatred for her. Elves hated all humans, especially sorcerers. Finally, he spat in her direction and continued on his way. A few others were with him, and they all cast her distrustful glances.

If it weren't for Jerik, they would likely try to kill her. She returned to her house and stood in the doorway. There were only a few stone and mud houses in the village, usually reserved for the important people of the village like the Tribe Chief. Perhaps that was another reason Velent disliked her so much. She had one of the best homes in a village that was not her own.

The other homes were made of wooden poles and animal hides. Jerik had told her that this was because the elves used to migrate from place to place. They were fairly sturdy, but sometimes wind storms would come through and a few elves would have to rebuild their tents.

A horn sounded in the distance. Jovanna looked toward the origin. Whoever had sounded the horn was too far to be seen yet, but they had made their intent to enter the village known.

Several warriors, including Velent, went running toward the sound. He was full of pride. Jovanna smirked. He reminded her of herself at times.

Half an hour later, Velent and his warriors returned, escorting a robed figure and a procession of elves. Jovanna's curiosity piqued, she watched as they walked along the path through the city, heading to the Tribe Chief's home.

She spotted Jerik heading her direction. She closed her eyes in irritation. "Jovanna," he said, "come with me."

"What do you want, old man?" she growled.

"The Tribe Chief has called a meeting and he has requested my presence."

"And?"

Jerik's face grew serious. "Something out of the ordinary is occurring. I'd like you there as well."

She stared hard at him for several moments, then nodded in silence. "I will come," she answered. She followed him to the center of the village. Once a month, the entire village would gather and have a feast.

A large tent had been erected for the occasion. The next feast would be held in two days. The elves were already gathering under the tent as they approached. Jerik led her through the crowd and to a table that had been set up for the Tribe Chief. Tanil was there already with his war advisors.

Jovanna had only seen Tanil a few times, usually from a distance. He wasn't as open about his hatred for her as his son was, but he only allowed her to stay because of Jerik. For reasons unknown to her, Jerik was highly esteemed by the elf leader.

Jerik sat at the table with Tanil and the others, but Jovanna chose to stand behind them, leaning against one of the thick poles that held the tent up. The old man didn't ask much of her outside of his constant talking, so the fact that he asked her to attend this meeting bothered her. Did he think something was going to happen?

The villagers parted as the robed elf and his entourage came to the tent, escorted by Velent. He sat beside his father. The visiting elves were not offered chairs as they were not the hosts. Guests were not treated in the friendly manners that humans showed to one another. Another thing Jovanna liked about the elves; they were rude. Unlike Cygnus.

Cygnus. She hadn't thought about him in months. He was the leader of the wizard city Palindrom, and one of the few people that Jovanna didn't hate. She didn't like him, but he had taken her in and tried to teach her how to control her magic. In the end, however, even he feared her.

She realized suddenly the entire tent had gone silent. According to elven custom, the visitor would speak first. If the Tribe Chief decided he liked what the visitor said, they wouldn't kill him. Jovanna liked such brutality. It displayed power. Jerik said it was barbaric.

The robed elf's men had brought a large chest with them. "The contents of this chest are a gift to the village," he said. Tanil nodded once, the sign that what had been spoken was agreeable.

One of the visiting elves opened the chest. The villagers began murmuring all at once. Jovanna squinted. It was full of food. At any other time, this would not have meant anything. Yet this was not an ordinary time. They were experiencing a drought.

The Deadlands was mostly desert. Very few plants

grew there, but the ones that did served as the food source for the elven tribes. The rains had come less frequently than in past years, and crop raising was difficult enough *with* the rain. The crops were barely producing enough food to feed the village, so some of the warriors had taken up hunting.

Jovanna had seen earlier the results of that endeavor. Velent and his men had returned with only a few quail and a malnourished addax. It seemed that the drought was affecting the animals of the desert as well.

"This is a generous gift," Tanil said. "All the tribes are dealing with the hardship of the drought. Where did this food come from? And why do you bring it to us and not share it with your own tribe?"

The robed elf waved his hand at the gathered villagers. "Are we not all Elves of the Tribe? We may live in different villages, and we may war against each other, but why should we not band together in this time of great difficulty?"

Tanil looked impressed. Jovanna could see Velent wasn't so easily convinced.

"There is more where this came from," the visitor said. "Much more. And it can be easily had. We only need to go out and retrieve it."

"And where is this food?" Velent said. Tanil scowled at his son. "Don't disgrace the gift," the Tribe Chief commanded. Velent sat back in his chair and folded his arms. "We are not beggars, father."

The robed elf nodded his head. "I take no offense at the question. I would have the same reservations if I was in your seat." The elf began speaking to the crowd. "Who is responsible for our troubles?" he asked. "Who drove us from our homes and into the Deadlands to fight for everything?"

"The humans!" one of the villagers shouted.

"Exactly!" the visitor said. "The humans drove us

from our homes and took our lands. They pushed us into this wasteland and grow fat off the land that is rightfully ours." The robed elf turned his attention back to Tanil. "The food is in the human lands. In *our* lands. It is time we unite and take back what is ours!"

Jerik gave Jovanna a look of alarm. The villagers started talking excitedly.

"What must we do to get this food?" Tanil asked.

"Swear your allegiance to me. Give me authority over your warriors and I will ensure the provision of your people."

"We reject your offer," Velent said, shaking his head. "What you ask for is foolish."

Tanil slammed his fist onto the table. Everyone turned their eyes to him. "Velent, you are not Tribe Chief. If you speak out of turn again, I will banish you from the tent."

Jovanna could see Velent was fuming. He kept his mouth shut, however.

"It sounds easy, but what you propose is unachievable," Tanil said. "Perhaps if more tribes were behind this cause, I would consider—"

The robed elf cut him off. "Every tribe has committed their warriors to me. You are the last tribe remaining."

"Impossible," Tanil replied. "The tribes have never been united, even before we were driven to the desert. Where is your proof?"

The visitor snapped his fingers. The elves who had traveled with him stepped forward, each one reciting their name and their tribe. When they finished, Jovanna had counted one elf for each of the major tribes. Tanil was quiet for a moment. "And if I refuse to commit?"

"That would not be wise, for you or your people."

Velent bristled at the threat. "Father," he said in hushed tones. "Do not let him strong arm you into this.

He could be lying."

Tanil ignored his son. "I will do as you say, so long as you promise my people will be taken care of." Velent stood up, his chair tumbling over behind him. "I will not bow to anyone but my father," he said.

"Velent, sit down!" Tanil shouted, outraged. Velent did not obey. He pointed to the robed elf.

"Warriors, seize him!" Several elves detached from the crowd and stalked toward the visitors.

The robed elf glowered at Velent. "You should reconsider your actions, *boy.* You don't know who you are angering."

Velent didn't answer. The warriors closed in and attempted to grab the visitors. Jovanna was amazed at the quickness of the robed elf's men. They unsheathed their swords and fought back against the warriors. Chaos ensued.

The war advisors leaped over the table, attempting to help their warriors subdue the visitors. The robed elf's men were cutting the warriors down left and right. Tanil seemed lost for a moment, then drew his own blade and flipped the table over. He and Velent joined the fray.

Jovanna found it all very amusing. They were fighting over something that was impossible. Elves invading human lands? She laughed at the thought. Jerik retreated beside her.

"This is not good," he said to her. She snorted.

"They will fight it out and the winner will get what they want. Such is the way of things."

Jerik shook his head. "You don't understand."

Be that as it may. She didn't care, either.

Tanil fell to the ground, wounded. Velent touched one of his tattoos and the ink flared to life with blue light. A thunderous *boom* shook the ground. One of the robed elf's men fell to the ground, charred by the magical explosion. Velent went flying backward as the robed elf countered back with his own spell.

One of the visitors stood over Tanil. With a nod from the robed one, the elf stabbed his sword into Tanil's throat, killing him.

Velent staggered to his feet, crying out in anguish. The robed elf went in for the kill. He raised his sword and thrust it forward.

A clang of metal sounded.

Jovanna's sword was a blur of motion. Her blade weaved a dangerous path through the air, parrying the blow of the robed elf. She knelt down and spun around, her foot lashing out and connecting solidly with a kneecap, sending the elf sprawling onto the ground as his leg gave out.

She leveled the blade with his throat. Lifting her left hand up, she called the magic to her. She 'saw' the magic floating all around her and commanded it to obey her will. Tendrils of black smoke began to rise from her hand, snaking through the air like tiny serpents.

The lithe lines of smoke angled down toward the elf, slowly wrapping around his legs. The magical haze tightened its grip on him as it tangled around his entire body, immobilizing him. Her eyes flickered momentarily, and the smoke began to change color to a reddish hue.

The elf grunted in pain as the smoke began to burn his flesh. She urged the tendrils to burn more intensely. The elf looked at her and she could see hatred boiling within him.

"*Sadaka lae nash!*" the elf shouted. The tendrils of smoke burst apart, scattering into the air. He struggled to his feet and snarled at her. His hood fell back, revealing his face. Jovanna thought she had seen him somewhere before.

He rolled his sleeve back and touched one of his tattoos. It came to life with blue light. He began to shimmer, then a popping sound filled the air and he was gone, leaving his men behind.

Jovanna laughed, thrilled with the excitement of battle. "Weakling!" she hollered. "He fled like a scared—" her words halted as she turned to see Jerik slumped up against a wooden tent pole.

He was dead.

—Jerik

CHAPTER 4

Twelve Years Ago

She watched the dog from a distance. Had it caught her scent? She couldn't know. She hadn't seen any other kids today. That was odd. Usually, there were a few others who walked this same section of the dump. They could have died. It wasn't out of the ordinary. The dump was a place of hard living, fighting for food, and always trying to stay warm at night.

She pulled her handmade dagger out of her belt just in case. She looked it over, making sure it was sharp enough to puncture flesh if she had to fight. She had made it out of a bone she found. By rubbing it against a rock, she had given it a fairly spikey point.

The dog perked its ears and she held her breath. She watched as the mutt sniffed the air and turned its attention elsewhere. She breathed out deeply and watched the dog until it disappeared among the mounds of trash. Only when she was sure it was gone did she come out of hiding. She still didn't see any other children. Shrugging, she continued searching through the trash for scraps.

She didn't know what city she lived in, but she knew it was big. The amount of trash in the dump told her that. The dump was massive, stretching as far as she could see in every direction. It was located on the southern end of the city, next to the slums. If only she lived in the slums. One could dream.

"Jovanna!"

She whirled around, pointing the dagger towards the voice. She sighed with relief when she saw it was only Danica. "You scared me," Jovanna said indignantly. Danica skipped over to her. She was always so happy.

"Sorry," she said. "I've never seen you scared before. You are the bravest kid I've ever met."

"*Psh*," Jovanna slapped the air and shook her head. "Just because I don't look scared doesn't mean I'm not scared on the inside. You find anything today?"

"I found this," Danica said, pulling a leftover piece of bread out of her pocket. She held it up for Jovanna to see. There were obvious teeth marks in it. She always wondered why people threw perfectly good food away.

"You are lucky," Jovanna said, smiling. "I haven't found anything yet." She turned and continued looking. Sometimes she touched things that made her shudder, but you had to look everywhere if you hoped to find something edible.

"Have you been to the pond today?" Danica asked, humming a tune as she followed Jovanna.

"No," she answered, realizing suddenly that she was pretty thirsty. The pond was the most dangerous place in the dump. It was the only source of water, and you had to be careful how much you drank. It would make you sick, causing stomach cramps so bad it would immobilize you, usually resulting in the dogs getting you.

Thankfully Jovanna had never gotten sick from the water. She was careful about not drinking too much, even though she wanted more. "Have you seen any others today?" she asked Danica. There was a pause.

"Now that you say that, I haven't. They could be dead."

"That's what I thought earlier," Jovanna said, pushing aside something wet and smelly. She scrunched her face in disgust but was rewarded with finding a piece of bread like Danica's. Whatever the wet smelly stuff was, it had gotten on the bread a little. "I need to go to the pond to wash this off," Jovanna informed Danica. "I'll see you later?" she asked.

Danica shrugged. "I'll come with you."

"Are you sure?" No one ever went to the pond twice. It was dangerous enough just trying to go once. She nodded. Jovanna led the way through the hills of trash, twisting and turning like giant snakes laid out in the sun. Snakes were a rarer occurrence in the dump, but Jovanna had come across one before. It was the best meal she could remember.

They walked for a long time. Every time they passed one of the safe areas—mini caves dug into the trash mounds or pieces of wood turned into shacks—they called out and glanced inside to see if any other kids were inside. Oddly, there weren't. Jovanna began to worry something bad, something very bad, must have happened.

The pond was surrounded by a tall circular wall of trash with one way in. Jovanna paused cautiously at the entrance and peered around the wall. No dogs. No kids, either. "It's safe," she said to Danica. They walked toward the water, glancing around the towering walls to make sure there weren't any animals hiding. Especially dogs. The dogs were vicious.

They approached the edge of the pond and Jovanna dipped her bread in and pulled it out quickly, then rubbed the nasty stuff off. It looked better so she took a bite out of it. It was a little moist from the water, but it was better than going to sleep hungry. "One day we are going to live in the slums," she promised Danica while chewing.

Danica was humming that tune she always sang. "That day will be great," she replied, her smile enveloping her face. A commotion rang out across the water. Jovanna snapped her gaze toward the noise. There, at the very back end of the pond, was a pack of dogs and a group of kids.

"What's happening?" Danica asked, squinting to see.

Jovanna was trying to determine that herself. "Let's get a closer look."

"I don't know … I think we should leave." Danica sounded scared. Jovanna didn't blame her. She didn't like the idea of being anywhere near a pack of dogs, but if they were fighting over food …

"Come on," Jovanna said. "I'll protect you." Danica nodded hesitantly. They walked along the edge of the pond slowly, not wanting to draw attention. After several minutes, they got close enough to see what was happening.

A deer carcass, freshly killed, was the object of the fight. The kids were fighting the dogs for the food. And they were losing. Jovanna could see several small bodies lying on the ground, dead or dying. This was bad. "It looks like they need help," Jovanna said.

Danica shook her head. "We need to leave. We can't stay here." Jovanna was debating what to do. Help the other kids drive the dogs back for the food, or run. Her instincts told her to run, but she didn't want to abandon the kids who needed help. The last few kids gave up the fight. They turned and fled, some of them scrambling up the hills and others running toward Jovanna and Danica.

"Let's go," Jovanna said, pushing Danica in front of her. She trotted backward for a few steps, watching the dogs. Some of them didn't stay with the deer. They were following the kids.

"Run!"

"Our character is constantly tested. The most difficult tests happen all at once."

—The Prophet of Edria

CHAPTER 5

Aramis dipped his mangled hand into the river. The water was surprisingly cold. He pulled it out a few seconds later after his hand had numbed. He rested it on his leg and let the air dry his skin.

"You aren't really a noble from … wherever you said then, are you?"

Mel nodded. "I am of noble blood, yes. And that is my family's estate. I have not seen them since I joined the order, though. I came here under the instruction of the Prophet."

"Who is the Prophet?" Aramis asked.

"He is the head of Edria's following. He alone receives divine counsel from her and guides the rest of us in her will."

"And Edria is …?"

Mel sighed. "Have you paid so little attention to what I have said? She is the Goddess of Knowledge."

Aramis held his hand up and inspected his broken fingers. At least the pain was manageable now. Before … Aramis shuddered. Jarn was a cruel man.

"The priests of my order can heal your hand," Mel informed him. "It would be wise of us to head there now, considering our current situation. If anyone sees you, they'll be sure to alert the guards."

"I can't go like this," Aramis replied, waving at himself. "I look like a vagrant. I need shoes and a shirt, at least. These pants will make do if I can wash the blood out of them."

"Of course, my Prince. I will go immediately and find you something."

"How are you going to do that?" Aramis asked. "You can't exactly go into the city. The guards will be looking for you as well. You assaulted soldiers. That's a serious crime unless you have forgotten?"

Mel frowned and tapped his chin with his index finger. "Blast. I had a perfect pair of Cantabrian albarcas and a brown silk tunic that would make you the envy of everyone. If neither of us can be seen, how do we get you something to wear?"

Aramis tensed as he heard a noise that sounded like a carriage. "Guards?" he asked, rising quickly to his feet. They were off the road, but the trees they were resting under were in plain view of anyone passing by.

"I don't think so," Mel answered, peering through the low hanging branches. "It would appear to be a cart. Yes, it is. And a woman is pushing it. We should stay here until she passes, just in case."

Aramis nodded in agreement. He watched as the rough looking cart trundled into view. A woman dressed in what appeared to be dirty rags stitched together walked behind it, pushing the cart with stooped shoulders. A hood covered her head and she walked barefoot.

A homeless woman, Aramis supposed. It seemed like the woman was going to pass by, but then she stopped when she reached the thicket of trees he and Mel were resting under.

She stood there, motionless. Without turning to look in their direction, the woman said: "Ah, Prince Aramis. And Melchiades. I knew he would guard you well. A shame about your father. I rather liked him."

Against his better judgment, he called out to the woman. "You knew my father?"

"My Prince," Mel whispered, shaking his head.

"Don't worry about me, Melchiades. I have no desire to see Aramis harmed." The woman turned her heard toward them. A dirty cloth covered her eyes, and Aramis realized she was blind. "I knew your father, though he did not know me. But that is not important."

She slid open a door on the top of the cart and rummaged through it. Finally, she pulled something out. Walking slowly and using a staff for support, she joined them under the shade of the willow trees. She held a bundle out for someone to take.

Aramis stepped closer and accepted it hesitantly. Unrolling it, he realized it was a shirt wrapped around a pair of shoes. "Thank you," he said gratefully. "How did you know I needed these?"

"Some things don't require sight, my boy."

"I am indebted to you. Mel, please pay her for these items."

She shook her head. "I don't want your money. They are a gift. You two must leave here quickly. A company of soldiers travel this road looking for you and will pass by shortly. Listen to me carefully. Trust Melchiades, for he will not lead you astray. The new king will not rest until he finds you."

"What new king? I am the heir." Aramis shook his head. "What are you talking about?"

"You will not understand everything now, but revelation will come in time. Now hurry, before the soldiers come." She turned and walked away, leaving Aramis troubled by her words. She reached her cart and continued pushing it along the road.

"We should cross the river," Mel said, interrupting his thoughts. "It might aid us in losing our pursuit. Then we will travel to my temple. You will be safe there. And perhaps my order can discern who the assassin was."

Aramis sighed. "I don't like the idea of leaving my people without a leader, but until I clear my name I have little choice in the matter."

"Thinking like a king already," Mel smiled at him.

Aramis decided not to put on the clothes the woman had given him until he dried off from crossing the river. Mel led the way, jumping onto exposed rocks to keep from getting soaked. About halfway across the river, they ran out of rocks. Mel turned to him. "Looks like we will have to get wet after all."

A *whirring* sound filled the air, followed by a splash. They turned simultaneously to see a group of five soldiers at the edge of the river behind them. They all had crossbows brandished and aimed.

"Go!" Mel shouted, grabbing Aramis by the shoulder and shoving him. "Get to the other side!"

Aramis didn't have much choice as the momentum from Mel's shove sent him flying into the cold water. Aramis instinctively sucked in his breath, along with some water, and started coughing. He ignored the burning in his throat and started swimming. He almost dropped his clothes. He glanced over his shoulder to see if Mel was following. The air rippled around him and that strange armor formed out of mist.

Aramis snapped his gaze forward and kept swimming. Mel would be fine. He reached the other side and sloshed out of the water, shivering. Even though it was summer, the water was freezing. He looked back at Mel again.

The soldiers were trying to shoot him down with their crossbows. Mel had summoned his sword and was deflecting the bolts out of the air. An occasional *clink* sounded. "Mel!" Aramis shouted. "Come on!"

Mel deflected two more arrows and then turned and leaped. Aramis expected him to sink like a rock, only he didn't. In fact, he didn't even appear to touch the water at all. Mel was running, his metal-clad feet barely rippling the surface of the water. Aramis stared, awestruck.

"Fancy trick," Aramis said as Mel stopped beside him. Melchiades grinned proudly. The air shimmered and then his armor was gone. An arrow slammed into the sandy ground at their feet. They exchanged looks and started running.

Several times Aramis stepped on rocks and other sharp objects. He cried out a few times as pain lanced through him, but kept going. They had to get out of range of the crossbows. They continued running for several minutes before stopping. They were both breathing hard and Mel was sweating.

Aramis noticed he wasn't cold anymore. He sat down on the ground and inspected the bottoms of his feet. There were numerous small cuts and sand clung to his skin. He brushed them off and put the shoes on. They were wet, but soft and felt good on his aching feet. He stood back up and put the shirt on as well. "Which way to the temple?" he asked.

Mel wiped the perspiration from his forehead and nodded to the east. "It's a two-day journey to Kaldore on foot. Perhaps we can find a carriage that will take us, or at least rent some horses."

"Let's do it quickly then. Before word gets too far that we are fugitives."

"Good point, my Lord."

● ∞ ● ∞ ●

Aramis leaned against the wall, arms crossed. He stared out a window, watching the clouds float lazily across the sky. In the distance, he could make out the sounds of a bustling town. The view was amazing, but he didn't recognize it. He suddenly realized he didn't know where he was.

He turned his attention to the room he was in. It was similar to his personal chambers in the castle, yet it was slightly different. Everything seemed to be in the right place, only ... it wasn't. He couldn't quite put his finger on it, but something was very wrong.

His left arm began to itch. He absently scratched it, then yelped in pain. There on his forearm was a black cross. "What the ..." he muttered softly. It was roughly the length of his middle finger and as wide as two.

He ran his finger along the shape and the flesh began to squirm under his touch. An intense fear made his stomach lurch. The black cross on his arm began to melt, small drops of black liquid falling to the floor.

There was no pain, just the incessant itching. The black drops began to drip faster, quickly pooling at his feet. He tried to rub the blackness off his skin but it seemed stuck, as though a part of his very flesh. Aramis watched in amazed shock as the black pool of liquid began to shift and take shape.

The cross disappeared as the last few drops fell from his arm. He staggered back from the shifting pool, his mind telling him to run. His body wouldn't obey him. A dark robed form rose from the black liquid of the floor.

The air in the room seemed to chill. Aramis could feel the hairs on his body stand on end. The figure turned toward him. The light in the room dimmed considerably and Aramis couldn't make out any of the person's features.

"I see the world cloaked in flame," the voice that came from the man was unearthly. It gave Aramis the impression of evil things scurrying in the darkness. Dead things. "And a sword will swiftly follow. My sword."

The figure was suddenly standing before him and the stench of rotting flesh reached his nostrils. He gagged, covering his mouth and nose with his hands.

"Who are you?" Aramis breathed.

"Mordum, God of the Dead."

Aramis startled awake, screaming and clutching his left arm in pain. Melchiades was standing over him, the concern evident on his face.

"My Lord," he asked hesitantly. "Are you well? I heard you screaming from the other room."

Aramis writhed in pain. His arm was burning like hellfire.

"Let me see it," he vaguely heard Mel say. He heard other voices as well and saw other people enter the room, men dressed similarly to Mel. He didn't know what he was doing or what was happening.

Brief images flashed through his mind. Men trying to hold him down. Mel's penetrating eyes staring at him. All swirled together with the haunting images of his dream.

And then the pain was gone. His mind cleared and he realized that he was tied down to the bed. Mel stood nearby, slowly flipping through pages in a book.

"What happened?" he asked.

Mel looked at him, offering a wan smile. "I wondered when you would come to. Forgive me for rapping you on the head, but after you struck the second priest, I had to do something."

"You knocked me out?" Aramis asked, surprised.

Mel nodded. "We have a lot to talk about. Why didn't you tell me you bore the mark?"

Aramis was confused. "The mark? What mark?" He tried to move but his bindings held him fast. "And untie me, will you?"

Mel complied with his request. Aramis sat up and ran his hands through his hair. "Now, what are you talking about?" Mel pointed to his arm. Aramis followed his gaze and his eyes widened in horror. A black cross, identical to the one in his dream, was on his left arm.

Aramis jumped up off the bed. "That was in my dream! Where is he?" He looked around the room frantically, but Mel was the only one in the room with him.

"Your dream? You dreamed of this symbol?" Mel asked.

"I wouldn't call it a dream so much as a nightmare." Aramis related the disturbing details. Mel listened in silence, seeming thoughtful.

"I remember something else," Aramis said. "The assassin who killed my father, he pointed at me and said something I didn't understand. I … I think that's when my arm started burning. Everything was so chaotic and fast, I honestly can't remember."

"I assume you don't know what this symbol is then, do you?"

Aramis shook his head. "I've never seen it before."

"This is the symbol of Mordum, the God of the Dead. The same figure who spoke to you in your dream."

"Why is this god's symbol on my arm?" Aramis asked.

"Why indeed," Mel replied. "I will need to speak with the Prophet about this. Perhaps he knows the answer. You should get some rest while I wait to speak to him. You look …"

"Horrible?"

"I was going to say tired, my Lord."

Aramis smiled at his friend. "I will try. Wake me when you know anything."

"Immediately," Mel said with a flourished bow before leaving him.

"Always the aristocrat," Aramis muttered. He looked around the room again to make sure the dark figure really was only a part of his dream, then he climbed back into the bed and closed his eyes.

He didn't sleep much.

—Prince Aramis

CHAPTER 6

Aramis sat on a stone bench in the hallway, waiting on Mel. While he didn't get much rest, he did feel more refreshed. The church had a bathing room which he had taken full advantage of. He'd shaved and cleaned up, as well as washed the blood from his pants. Laying in a bed had been a welcome reprieve from the cramped carriage they had ridden in to get to the temple.

Now he waited impatiently for Mel to finish speaking with the Prophet. Most of the other priests seemed to keep their distance from him. He first thought was that it was because they knew he was the king, but Mel informed him it was because of the mark on his arm. Apparently, Mordum was the sworn enemy of Edria.

Aramis didn't care about their religious politics. He just wanted the thing removed and his hand healed, which still no one had done. He needed to hunt down the man who had killed his father so he could clear his name and claim the throne.

The words of the blind woman from the castle still bothered him. Who was she talking about when she said 'the new king'? The nobles might be petty and fight amongst themselves, but none of them would try to usurp the throne. Or would they?

His troubled thoughts were interrupted as a door opened and Mel stepped into the hallway. He stood there for a moment and covered his face with his hands. Mel appeared more troubled than Aramis felt. Mel lowered his hands and stopped midway, seeming surprised to see Aramis. "What are you doing here?" he asked.

"I thought I would wait here for you," Aramis answered. "Is there a problem?"

Mel shook his head. "Of course not," he answered, his entire demeanor changing. "I was simply curious. Come," he beckoned Aramis with his hand.

Aramis rose and followed Mel down the corridor and out into the open courtyard of the church. Priests were moving in all directions, most of them carrying parchments. They wove their way through the bustling courtyard and out into the city of Kaldore. The church of Edria was located inside the city, surrounded by a short wall that was more for decoration than any sort of defense.

"What did the Prophet say?" Aramis finally asked. "Is he going to remove this mark?"

Mel didn't answer immediately. "He said he is not able to."

"Who can?"

"He doesn't know if it *can* be removed. The mark of Mordum is given to his agents when they swear their devotion to him. A commitment to Mordum is for life, and his followers carry the mark until they die." They stopped beside an abandoned building, its windows and doors boarded up.

"I'm not a follower of this Mordum," Aramis said

indignantly.

"I know that," Mel replied, "But the Prophet does not. He won't allow anyone to heal your hand until you agree to something first. Something that will prove you are not an agent of Mordum."

"Are you jesting with me?" Aramis asked.

"I wish that were the case, my Lord. Things have changed dramatically, it seems. There are many things unfolding not just in your kingdom, but in others. The Prophet believes these events are all linked to Mordum. His followers are moving quickly to secure important positions all over the lands. I had hoped the Prophet would take my word for your testimony. Unfortunately, since I was not in your father's room with you when the assassin struck, he cannot trust you based on my word alone." Mel sighed and leaned back against the building.

They both sat in silence, watching the townspeople pass. "I suppose whatever he requests of me shouldn't be too difficult. If my arm wasn't defaced with this mark, then he would believe me. Wouldn't he?"

"I don't know. He will not ask anything easy of you, that I am sure of. He did not tell me what your task would be, he only told me to see what your answer would be."

Aramis chewed on his lower lip. "What other option do I have? I cannot go back to the castle until my name is cleared, and I can't do that so long as my father's killer is walking freely. I need proof I didn't do it. Tell your prophet I will do it."

One of the townspeople approached them pushing a wooden cart. Aramis assumed it was a vendor coming over to try and sell them something. He was about to tell the person they weren't interested when he realized it was the blind woman from the castle.

"Prince Aramis," she greeted as she reached them. She halted pushing the cart. "I see you two escaped the soldiers. Good thing I warned you." She smiled at them.

Aramis stared at the cloth that covered her eyes. "You aren't really blind, are you?" he asked.

"Of course I'm blind," she cackled. "Why would you think otherwise?"

"You recognized us back at the castle. And just now you said you 'see' we escaped the soldiers. And how did you get here so fast? We rented a carriage and got here yesterday. There's no way you pushed that cart all the way here in so short a time."

The lady continued to smile, but she reached up and removed the cloth. Aramis' mouth dropped. Where the woman's eyes should have been were two empty sockets. "You see?" she asked. "I am as blind as it gets."

"But how …?" Aramis trailed off, dumbfounded.

"I told you before, some things don't require sight." She tied the cloth back in place, then reached into her cart and shuffled through it. Aramis and Mel exchanged looks but didn't say anything. Finally, she pulled out a dagger. She held it out for Aramis to take. "You'll need this. It's the only thing that will work."

Aramis accepted the weapon. He turned it over in his hands. It had a plain wooden hilt. The blade itself was only a few inches long and seemed likely to rust soon. He looked to Mel who shrugged in response. "I'll need it for what?" he asked.

"You'll see in time," she answered nonchalantly. "I must be on my way now. Remember what I said about Melchiades?" she asked.

"Trust him," Aramis answered. She nodded once and continued pushing her cart.

"There's something really odd about that woman," Aramis said as he slid the dagger into his belt. Mel watched her closely as she left.

"I couldn't agree more."

● ∞ ● ∞ ●

A few hours later, Aramis was summoned to speak with the Prophet. Mel escorted him to the same hallway they had previously been in. His friend knocked on the door and another priest answered. He looked to be the same age as Mel. They entered into a small room with no chairs or decorations of any kind. Aramis waited with Mel while the other priest disappeared through another door.

"He's going to let the Prophet know you are here. The first time someone meets him, it can be a little nerve-wracking. He can be … overzealous."

Aramis wasn't worried. He grew up in the king's court. After a few minutes, the priest returned and led them into the Prophet's chamber. The room was windowless, but candles were everywhere. Aramis assumed there must have been hundreds of them. They gave the room an eerie yellowish-orange glow. He could smell something in the air. Probably incense.

Behind a large wooden desk stood the Prophet. He didn't look how Aramis had pictured. He was tall, with broad shoulders and a muscular frame. He had black hair, or at least it appeared black in the lighting. Aramis couldn't tell. He wore robes similar to Mel's, though they were much more richly decorated. A large gold chain hung from his neck with a pendant of a closed hand with an open eye in the center. He'd seen that symbol etched on the back of Mel's armor; the symbol of Edria.

"Welcome Prince Aramis," he greeted formally. Aramis bowed in respect. "Please sit down. We have a lot to talk about." There was only one chair in front of the Prophet's desk. Aramis looked to Mel, who motioned him to take the seat. Aramis did so. He leaned back and tried not to inhale the smoke from the candles on the desk.

If the Prophet noticed his discomfort, he didn't say anything. "Melchiades says that despite the fact that you wear the mark of Mordum, you are not one of his agents. I'm a logical man. If you don't belong to Mordum, why do you have the mark?" He leaned forward, the shadows of the candlelight wavering along his face.

"I do not know for certain how I got it, but I have not devoted myself to Mordum, let alone any other god. I am not a weakling to rely on fairy tales to get me through life."

He looked at Mel. "No offense." Mel nodded, knowing Aramis didn't put faith into anything other than what he could see.

"What I do know is that my father was killed by a man who managed to scale the castle walls despite the fact that they are warded against magic. He said something to me I didn't understand, and then he simply disappeared into thin air. I haven't even had time to properly grieve my father's passing. I am a fugitive in my own kingdom for a crime I didn't commit. I've come to hear your request of how to prove that I am not a follower of Mordum, not to sit here as though I am on some sort of trial when I could be searching for the assassin who killed my father!"

Aramis ended his tirade, suddenly feeling like a fool. The Prophet could give him the opportunity he needed to clear his name, and he just yelled at the man. His emotions had gotten the better of him. He was about to apologize when the Prophet sat back and smiled.

"Your father certainly raised you to speak like a king. I understand your position, but you have to understand mine. Let me explain." The Prophet stood up and walked over to a table in the corner of the room. Mel nudged Aramis and nodded toward the table. Aramis stood and joined the Prophet. "This is a map of everything that has ever been explored. My predecessor had it commissioned for missionary purposes. Today it serves me as a means to track the enemies of my goddess."

The Prophet pointed to Talvaard. "We know that a follower of Mordum wages a war here in disguise, but we have yet to figure out who it is. Here," he moved his finger to the Deadlands, "another is trying to organize the elven tribes under one banner. We don't know why, but I'm not as concerned about that." He pointed to Oakvalor. "Here is your kingdom. The king is murdered, by *you* according to the word spreading, and you bear the mark of Mordum.

"His followers have been dormant for years. Now they are moving to secure entire cities. In Talvaard, they are moving to secure an entire kingdom. Aside from the fact that Mordum is Edria's enemy, this is cause for concern even for those who don't believe in fairy tales," he said, looking directly at Aramis. "Mordum is God of the Dead. He seeks to destroy life and anything that is good. If whatever he is planning comes to pass, I can guarantee that we will all suffer the consequences."

"What does all of this have to do with me?" Aramis asked.

"As of right now, I believe you are the agent of Mordum in Oakvalor. So unless you can give me proof that you are not, I have no other choice but to assume I am right."

Aramis considered the implications of what the Prophet was saying. "What do you want me to do to prove that I'm not?"

The Prophet turned back to the map and pointed to the Viss Mountains. "There is a shrine to Mordum in these mountains. Once a year, his followers gather there to collect blood that comes out of the shrine. When they drink it, it gives them power. I don't know where the blood comes from or how it gives his followers power, but we do know the time for the next collection is coming. I want you to retrieve this blood and bring it back to me."

Aramis frowned. "What are you going to do with it? And why can't your priests get it for you?"

"Fair questions," the Prophet said. "My spies tell me that some kind of ritual is going to happen, and the blood from this shrine is one of the keys to the ritual. If you are not truly a follower, you will have no qualms about getting this and bringing it to me. As to why my priests cannot gather this blood, that is because only those who have the mark of Mordum can enter the gate surrounding the shrine."

"What if they realize I'm not one of them and they try to kill me? This doesn't seem like a fair deal."

The Prophet chuckled. "Who said this was a deal? You are in a bind, Aramis. I could execute you as a follower of Mordum, or turn you in for crimes against the country. You have a tough decision to make, but it is your decision."

"Suppose I do this task and I am successful, thus proving I am not a follower of this god Mordum. What benefit do I get from this that will help me clear my name?"

The Prophet stared at him intently. "You will have the backing of Edria and her church. I will issue an edict declaring our belief in your innocence, and I will provide you with anything you need to catch the real assassin.

"What say you?" the Prophet asked.

Aramis scratched his chin. "I will do it," he decided.

CHAPTER 7

Jovanna followed Danica to the first safe area, a small cave dug into the trash. She didn't see any of the other kids now. They all ran in different directions. She could hear the dogs barking not too far behind them.

"We won't be able to fend them off here," Jovanna said as Danica was started to climb through the entrance. "The opening is too big. We need somewhere that only one dog can come in at a time if they find us."

Danica hesitated. She was scared and just wanted to hide. Jovanna didn't fault her for that. But they had to be smart about it. If you didn't think smart, you didn't live long. Jovanna grabbed Danica's hand and pulled her out of the cave, dragging the younger girl behind her. She kept her bone dagger in her free hand, clutching it tightly.

Her mind raced through the many places they could hide. Which one would be best? The dogs were getting closer. She didn't have much time to choose, and she had even less time to get wherever she chose. And then she had an idea.

"Faster!" she yelled at Danica. She veered to the left, towards where she found the bread. The smelly wet stuff she had encountered, if they rubbed it on themselves, would hinder the dogs from being able to smell them. The idea of rubbing that nasty stuff on her skin was repulsive, but desperation called for options that weren't normally considered.

They reached the area fairly quickly. Jovanna continued pulling Danica behind her as they climbed the steep hill of garbage. "Here," she said breathlessly. "Roll around in it." Jovanna pointed.

Danica had a look of utter disgust on her face. "No way," she said defiantly. "I don't want that on me."

"Do you want the dogs to find you?"

Danica looked over her shoulder to where the dogs would be coming, then back to the slime. She closed her eyes, pinched her nose, and fell face first into the smelly stuff. Jovanna did the same, rolling around and feeling the slime cover her skin. Her body involuntarily shuddered at the feeling.

"Gross, gross, gross," she heard Danica whispering.

"Quiet!"

Danica stopped talking and Jovanna listened intently. She didn't hear anything. Perhaps the dogs had lost their trail. Jovanna decided, to be safe, they would wait for a while before moving. She lay there in the slime, listening. She felt like forever had passed before she finally lifted her head to look around. *No sign of the dogs.*

She turned to Danica to let her know it was okay to move, but the girl had fallen asleep. Jovanna smiled at the sight. Danica's blonde hair was stained a brownish green color from the slime. Her tattered clothing barely hung to her body. Where the material had completely ripped, she had tied it back together with small knots. Danica was already living in the dump before Jovanna came to call it home.

Jovanna had been here two years now. She couldn't believe how much time had gone by when she really thought about it. Two long, grueling years of fighting merely to survive. At least at the orphanage, she was guaranteed real food. Not much, but it was still more than she found now.

The orphanage.

Before the dump, she lived at an orphanage for a few weeks. Before that, she had a real family. Her parents had loved her. That was before …

No.

She pushed the thoughts from her mind. She dared not think about that time. She slowly got to her feet, trying to be as quiet as possible so as not to wake Danica. She stood there in silence, looking across the dump. She didn't see or hear any sign of the dogs. She sighed and tried not to breath in the smell of the slime covering her.

She would be forced to wash in the pond. She hadn't taken a bath in several weeks. It was hard to find a safe time to do so. She slid the bone dagger into her belt and climbed down the hill. She wouldn't leave Danica unprotected, but she needed to find more food. She had dropped the bread she found when they fled the pond.

Jovanna started picking through the trash. People threw lots of things away. Every once in a while she would find a coin or two. When most of the other kids found coins, they would go to the slums and spend them on food or clean water.

Not Jovanna. While it was tempting to use them, especially when she couldn't find anything to eat, she saved them. She hid them across the dump, always careful not to put too many in one spot. She also hid them in spots that didn't get explored much.

Once she had enough coins, she was going to buy a shack in the slums. She was only eight, true, but several children had their own shacks. Either their parents had died, leaving them what little they owned, or their parents had simply abandoned them. No one really cared what happened in the slums. They cared even less about what happened in the dump.

She spotted something shiny and reached for it. Before her fingers could reach it, she heard a scream. She spun around, her heart suddenly racing. Her eyes scanned the hill.

There.

Danica was running from a dog. Not just any dog. The dog she saw earlier before Danica met up with her. The mangy mutt easily overtook Danica, snapping at her heel and tripping her in the process. Jovanna sprinted toward them, her skinny legs burning from the effort of trying to run through the garbage that seemed to try and suck her down.

Jovanna growled in frustration and used her hands to aid in her climb. She finally reached Danica. She was in a frantic fight with the dog. It was all snapping teeth, growls, and blood.

Lots of blood.

Jovanna jumped into the fray, using her bone dagger to stab the dog several times. The animal's growls turned to cries of pain. The dog tried to turn and bite her, but she jumped backward out of the way and kicked the dog in the jaw. The dog yelped in response but attacked her still.

She fell to the ground as the dog slammed into her. She momentarily freaked out. She hated not being in control. The dog's nails raked across her flesh, opening wounds along her arms. Jovanna pushed her left arm up to try and block the dog while angling her right arm to the side.

She screamed in pain as she felt the dog clamp down on her arm, the animal's teeth piercing her skin. She tried to keep her focus. She lifted her free arm and swung as hard as she could, bone dagger leading the way.

She was rewarded with a cry from the dog as well as the sensation of something warm spraying against her skin. The dog released her arm and ran, leaving a trail of blood behind. Jovanna lay there breathing heavily. She could hear her heartbeat in her ears. Was that normal?

Relief flooded over her as she realized that the cuts on her arm weren't very deep. That was good. It could have been much worse. She struggled to her feet and saw Danica laying very still.

Danica!

She had almost forgotten the girl she was trying to save in her frantic fight with the dog. "Danica, it's okay. The dog is gone. I stabbed him pretty good." She still didn't move. "Danica," Jovanna said as she knelt down beside the girl and grabbed her shoulder. She rolled the girl onto her back. Her heart fell into her stomach.

Danica's throat was ripped open. Blood covered the entire front of her body. Jovanna grit her teeth against the pain. She stood up and looked around. There was still no sign of the dogs from the pond. But the fresh scent of blood would easily draw them. *Well,* Jovanna thought, *they won't be making a meal out of this girl.*

Jovanna grabbed Danica's feet and pulled the girl's lifeless body behind her. There was a place nearby where the kids buried their dead. The dogs never went around it for some reason, which is why they picked the spot for their graveyard. Jovanna was angry at that stupid dog. Angry that another person had been robbed from her. Angry that life was so hard.

Warm tears spilled down her face. She cried for her fallen friend mostly. But she also cried for herself. She cried the entire time she pulled Danica's body behind her, the entire time she dug a hole in the graveyard for Danica's body, and the entire way back to her shelter. She cried until she finally fell asleep.

And that was the last time she cried.

—Melchiades

CHAPTER 8

Dusk had finally arrived. Jovanna wanted nothing more than for the day to end. She stood a short distance from the hut that Jerik had made his home. Two guards were posted at the doorway of the mud and stone building, mainly to keep curious children away. None of the elves dared to enter the makeshift tomb. They considered it a bad omen to stand in the presence of the dead.

They did, however, walk by and pause momentarily in front of the doorway. One at a time, everyone in the village—or so it seemed—stopped in silence, paying tribute in their own way to the man. Jovanna was conflicted. Death came to everyone at some point. That was a fact she had come to acknowledge long ago. And she didn't really care for the man. Yet Jerik's death bothered her. It was like a parasite eating at her mind.

She kept reminding herself that he had saved her life

and so she felt she owed him a debt of some kind. And now he was gone. If you owed something to another, did death break the debt? She didn't know the answer to that. She didn't know what she owed him, either.

So she just stood there staring at the darkened doorway for what felt like hours. She barely noticed when the ash stopped falling. Eventually, all of the villagers had paid their respects and went back to their normal routines. Even the guards left their post after night claimed the sky. A part of her wanted to go in there and look at him one last time. The other part of her wanted to burn the building down and forget she had ever met the man.

A voice inside told her this was what it meant to care. She scoffed at the thought. She didn't care about anyone or anything. She started to turn away and go to her own house when she heard shouting coming from the Tribe Chief's home. It sounded like Velent. She cast another glance to Jerik's house, then made her way toward the commotion.

When she reached the Tribe Chief's house, she expected to find an argument of some kind. She was disappointed when she saw otherwise.

"We must not let this traitor get away with his crimes," Velent was saying. She peered into the doorway. The leaders of the warriors and some of the tribe's elders were gathered in a circle, listening to Velent speak. Some of them were nodding their heads, others were shouting aggressively in agreement.

"I issue a formal declaration of war on the tribes responsible. I don't care if every tribe is gathered under one banner. I will go to the grave seeking justice."

Jovanna thought he was a fool. But as he continued with his speech, Jovanna began to understand what he was doing. By default, he was the new Tribe Chief. However, anyone could challenge him if they felt he was failing in his duty as the leader of the tribe.

He was bringing them to his cause, and by doing so, was earning their support to lead the tribe. Maybe she was wrong. Perhaps he was only slightly foolish.

"And what if we lose?" one of the elders spoke up. Immediate silence fell among the elves. "What then?"

Velent acknowledged the elder elf with a nod of his head. "It is a risk we must take. If we don't strike back for this crime, they will return again."

"Perhaps," the elder said. "What happens to our village if we lose? If all of our warriors are killed, what of our women and children? They will be defenseless against the other tribes. You know what will happen," he said ominously.

"I do," Velent said softly. "I have considered this already. And I have also put a plan into place should that be the case. Our people will be safe. I vow it."

Jovanna leaned against the wall beside the door and half listened to the rest. Velent went over his plan to track down the tribes responsible and what the villagers should do if they were to lose. He dismissed them and ordered them to get their rest. She waited until everyone left before stepping into the doorway.

"What are you doing here?" Velent demanded angrily.

Jovanna ignored his question. "I heard you've declared war on the other tribes," she said casually, looking at the few items that decorated the house.

"That's none of your concern," he answered. "So I ask again, what are you doing here?"

"It's no secret that we can't stand each other," she said. "But there is one thing we can agree on. The death of your father and of Jerik must be dealt with." Velent continued to glare at her but he didn't say anything.

"I want to go to war with you."

"You are not fighting with us," Velent replied. "You

are not an elf. You don't belong here."

Jovanna wanted to strangle him. "I want to be here less than *you* want me here, trust me. But if I do not fight to avenge Jerik's murder, how would I honor him? Stand by and do nothing?" Though the elven tribes were barbaric, they adhered to a strict code of honor. Jovanna appealed to that quality. "He saved my life," she reminded him.

"He saved many lives," Velent answered.

She scowled at him. *Impetuous brat.*

"Tradition forbids it. And unlike my father, I will not betray our customs. Out of respect for Jerik, you can stay in the village. For now. But I will not let you go to war with us. Even if you were of the tribe, our women do not fight. They tend to the children and the chores. Only men go to war."

And to think that she thought he was clever. "I can fight better than any of your men. And I can cast any spell you can. Stop giving me petty excuses. I'm willing to put my hatred for you aside to achieve a common goal. Can you not do the same, *boy?*"

She took satisfaction in seeing Velent's jaw stiffen. "I. Refuse." His tone implied finality. But Jovanna was stubborn. She crossed her arms and stared him in the eyes.

"Jerik saved my life," she reiterated. "I will go and avenge him. I have more right to do so than you. He was not an elf either. He was a man."

Velent shook his head in frustration. "You do not know what you speak of." He motioned toward the door. "Now leave."

Jovanna pushed him aside with her shoulder as she left. She wanted to punch him in the face. He could deny her the right to fight with them all he wanted, but he couldn't stop her from fighting the tribes herself. She hesitated as she passed Jerik's house. What would he do? She knew what he would say. He would have tried to dissuade Velent from war.

She was not Jerik. She grew up fighting for everything she needed. War was her life. If he had thought to change her, he was more foolish than Velent. She continued toward her house. She smiled as she began forming a plan. Velent would let her go to war if he didn't *know* it was her.

This was going to be perfect.

• ∞ • ∞ •

Jovanna was up before the sun rose. She had packed what few belongings she had into a small sack. It was made of long reeds tied together; a gift from one of the few elven women who spoke to her. It had a strap attached to it for carrying. She slung the strap over her shoulder. It felt heavier than it looked.

Grabbing her sword, she sheathed it in the left side of her belt. She doubted Velent would notice her sword was different than those of his warriors'. She had used a spell to change her appearance. She didn't have a mirror to check, but her illusion should have given her the visage of a young elven male. She wouldn't be able to speak, as even magic had its limitations.

She went back over the plan in her mind. She would join Velent's ranks as they marched out of the village and fight beside them against the other tribes. If the battle looked to be going ill for Velent, Jovanna would retreat and go her own way. If the battle went well, she would continue with them. She waited at her doorway and listened as the elves marched through the village.

They marched quickly and quietly, perhaps to keep from waking the rest of the village. She waited until the last warrior passed her house, then she stepped out onto the road and followed the small army. She couldn't see clearly enough to get a correct count, but she guessed Velent only had fifty warriors at his disposal. She had seen battles won with smaller forces, but they usually boasted cavalry. Elves didn't ride horses though, so the battle could go either way.

Every elf was tattooed from the neck down, making them all potent weapons. But if what the visitor had said was true, he had united the other tribes under one banner. There was something about that elf that didn't seem right. She couldn't figure it out, but that didn't really matter. He would fall to her blade as easily as her previous enemies had.

The elf in front of her looked over his shoulder at her and did a double take. Jovanna gritted her teeth, thinking her illusion had faded prematurely.

"I thought I was bringing up the rear," he said.

She shrugged her shoulders in response. It would be easy to keep from speaking while they marched, but she'd be forced to speak at some point. By then Velent wouldn't have any other choice but to let her fight.

"What do you think about this rumor?" he asked her. He wasn't looking at her, but she knew he had directed his question at her. She remained silent, hoping he'd just leave her alone.

"No one wants to talk about it," he continued, "but we should consider if it is true. If this elf has united the tribes, he has done a mighty thing. 'Who can stand against an elf? No one. Who can stand against all elves? No one.'"

Jovanna recognized that quote. Jerik had told her its meaning. Supposedly an ancient Tribe Chief from one of the clans had said that in a speech to rally his warriors. Elves saw themselves as the favored race above any other, despite their destitution and harsh living conditions. The elf continued to ramble, but Jovanna didn't pay him any attention.

She stared at the vastness that stretched out before them known as the Deadlands. It had been aptly named. The desert was an unforgiving place. There were more creatures that could kill with a single bite here than any other place she had been to. It was quite possibly on par with the dump she spent some of her childhood living in. Perhaps the only difference was that in the Deadlands there was more to eat, even with the drought.

She had lost track of how long they traveled, but they stopped when the sun was nearing the middle of the sky. All of the elves took a break, drinking water from skins and eating meager rations. Jovanna drank some water but refused to eat anything. She fought better on an empty stomach.

They rested for only a few minutes and then they were up and moving again. They didn't travel more than an hour when they stopped again. There was murmuring among the elves.

"We've found a village," the elf in front of her said, still not looking at her. He paused. "It appears to be empty."

Jovanna smirked. The elf must have known Velent would declare war and had the villages retreat somewhere safe.

"He knows we're coming," she said aloud to herself. The elf looked at her quizzically.

"What?"

Jovanna shook her head. She needed to be more careful. The elf turned back around. They waited a few more moments and then continued marching. Every half hour, almost like clockwork, they came across an empty village.

"It seems the rumor must be true," the elf said. "No tribe spaces their villages this closely together. Not even during an alliance."

She had been thinking the same thing. Her pulse

quickened at the anticipation of battle. They had passed through several villages now. They couldn't be far from whatever trap their enemy had set. And she knew they were walking into a trap. It was too obvious. Perhaps Velent knew that as well. Yet he still led them onward. She had to admit that he certainly didn't lack courage.

Energy began to thrum through her body as they continued. Something was going on ahead. She could feel the magic pounding against her flesh like the sound of war drums. She noticed the magic was erratic, not flowing rhythmically like it normally did. This was definitely a trap.

Jovanna unsheathed her blade, wanting to be ready. The elf in front of her looked at her oddly, but she didn't care. She scanned the landscape but didn't see anything out of the ordinary. Yet the magic continued to beat against her flesh. It was almost becoming painful. The elf in front of her broke away from them, pointing to a small patch of cacti.

"I'm going to relieve myself," he said.

She nodded and continued following the others. A few moments later, the elf returned. They entered another abandoned village, similar looking to the others. The magic was pulsing so strongly now Jovanna thought it might rip through her flesh.

She stopped walking and looked at the huts around her. They were made of the same materials as the ones in Velent's village. Nothing out of the ordinary. She stepped into one of them. It had a bed and some chairs made of reeds, but nothing more. She left the hut and walked to the next one, followed by the next one. The pulsing was getting stronger with every step she took. She had a feeling it was coming from one of the huts.

She entered the next hut. There, sitting on the bed, was an elf. His breathing was quick and shallow and he was covered in sweat. The tattoos on his skin were glowing fiercely. And he wasn't wearing any clothes. Not even a loincloth.

That didn't faze her, but his odd behavior did. That and the pulsing magic was coming from his body. His feverish eyes turned to her. They were bloodshot and had started to cloud over.

"What's wrong with you?" she asked softly. His body jerked wildly as he attempted to stand. Jovanna backed up, not sure what he was doing. Finally, the elf managed to get up, and with wild uneven movements, he made his way towards the door.

She continued to back up and exited the hut, watching him warily. She realized that some of the elves had noticed the naked elf and had come to investigate.

"What's wrong with him?" one of them asked her. She shrugged. She honestly didn't know, but the fact that his body was burning with energy wasn't a good sign.

One of the elves ran back to the others, probably to fetch Velent. Within moments the entire army had turned around and come back. Velent walked up to the man and touched his shoulder. He quickly pulled his hand away.

"His skin is on fire!" he said, clenching his hand. "Where are his clothes?"

No one spoke. Velent turned to the elf that had fetched him. "Where did you find him?" The elf said something softly in reply that Jovanna didn't hear.

The elf's tattoos began to pulse. His breathing remained shallow, but it was slowing down rapidly. His eyes were now completely covered in a thick milky substance. Velent called for one of the elders who made his way through the crowd of confused warriors.

"We must leave, now!" the elder yelled.

Velent stopped the elder with his hand. "What do you mean we have to leave? What's wrong with him?" The elder started ranting. Jovanna didn't understand most of it because he was talking too fast. She heard the word "stone-skin", which meant nothing to her.

The elf dropped to his knees and Jovanna noticed blood was starting to drip from his eyes. She had never seen *that* happen before. The elder pushed through the warriors and ran away quickly. She watched him run until she could no longer see him, then she looked back to Velent.

He was still investigating the naked elf. Jovanna could feel the magic thundering in her ears now. She vaguely heard something and looked to her right. The elf who had been marching in front of her was looking at her with concern.

She gave him an odd look. He pointed at her. She raised her hand and waved it, bidding him to say something.

"Your ears," he said.

She reached up and touched one but didn't feel anything. She looked at her fingers, thinking her ears might be bleeding with the pounding of the magic. Nothing. She looked at him questioningly.

"They are melting," he added.

A thunderous *boom* sounded and the next thing Jovanna knew, she was lying on her back staring up at the sun. Her ears were ringing and a foul smell was assaulting her nostrils. She sat up for a moment—just long enough to see the devastation—and fell back down.

Everyone was dead.

—Precept of Zevea

CHAPTER 9

Aramis stared through the black gates that guarded the shrine of Mordum. He was hiding beside Mel in the woods that surrounded the shrine, waiting and watching. The Prophet said it was reported that the blood would come out of the fountain at midnight.

They had barely found a caravan to travel with. Although the war with Talvaard was at a stand-still, most people still didn't travel across the border. Using a crudely drawn map, they had navigated the mountain trails to the shrine. They had seen the caved-in entrance of the tunnel Calderon had supposedly defeated Orlek in.

They'd been watching for over an hour and had yet to see anyone. It was almost midnight. Aramis looked to Mel. "It's almost time. I should get in there. Who knows how long the blood will be available in the fountain."

Mel summoned his armor and sword, the air rippling with mist around him. "I can't enter through the gates,

75

but I can keep others from going in. Be careful, my Lord."

Aramis walked over to the gate entrance. He took another look around and pushed the door. It swung open on silent hinges. *It's well maintained,* he thought. After he stepped through the gate, it swung shut behind him with a soft *clang*. He stood perfectly still, half expecting an army of Mordum's priests to come from every direction.

Nothing.

Stepping slow and quiet, he walked around the area looking for the fountain. Although the sky was clear, the moon didn't seem to illuminate anything. Everything was bathed in shadows. Trees looked like gnarled creatures, hanging vines looked like claws reaching to whisk him away into the darkness. He was about to go back when he saw a faint glow coming from a ring of trees. He approached cautiously.

Peering through a gap in the trees, he saw the glow was coming from a pile of neatly stacked rocks. They illuminated a rectangular stone roughly five feet wide by five feet tall. In the center was a carving of a horned creatures head. Its mouth was open in a silent roar and water poured from it into a round metal bowl. Circling around the trees, he entered the small clearing.

His arm began burning as he neared the fountain. He rubbed it unconsciously. If people came here to get the blood, where were they? Aramis knelt down in front of the shrine and looked into the metal bowl. The water was crystal clear. He didn't see a drain, so where would the water go once the bowl was full? He touched the ground expecting it to be damp. It was dry.

"Hmm," he muttered softly. "That's odd." He stood back up and examined the rest of the fountain. It was relatively plain except for the carved head. It was made from a shiny black rock, possibly obsidian. The eyes sparkled red. He leaned in closer and realized the eyes were rubies. They were a decent size, probably worth a small fortune. A rustling sound caught his attention.

Aramis pushed himself up against the trees that ringed the clearing and looked through one of the gaps. He didn't see anything, but he heard muffled voices. A sudden panic shot through him. He started wondering why he agreed to do the Prophet's work in the first place. He had to remind himself that he was trying to clear his name. The Prophet was the first step.

He turned back to the fountain when he heard the water sputtering. Water still came out of it, but it was tinged red. It continued to sputter for several moments before a thick red liquid replaced the water.

Blood. Aramis knew that's what he had come to collect, but part of him didn't believe blood would actually come from a fountain. It surprised him. He shook his head and pulled the wineskin he brought from his belt. Sudden shouts broke out across the clearing. Aramis hurriedly held the skin under the fountain, collecting the blood. He filled it most of the way and then capped it. He wrapped the strings through his belt, ensuring they were tight so the bag wouldn't come loose and fall.

He could hear the sounds of battle now. Mel was surely fighting the followers of Mordum who had come to gather the blood themselves. Aramis sprinted towards the gate. He didn't have a sword, but he was well trained in hand to hand. A movement to the left, from the corner of his eye, caught his attention. He didn't pay it any heed; he just kept running. And then a hissing sound filled the air. He looked over his shoulder just in time to see something large crash into him.

Snapping jaws tried to maul his face. He covered his head protectively with his arms, attempting to roll away from whatever it was. Sharp claws raked across his arms as the thing tried to get at his head. Aramis started swinging his fists wildly. One of his blows connected, hitting something hard and scaly. The thing hissed loudly and backed away. He scrambled to his feet, the wounds on his arms burning like fire.

It was too dark to tell what was attacking him. All he could see was a big shadow. It was coming back at him. He took off running back toward the fountain. The creature was right behind him. Whatever it was, it was quick. He heard the thing's jaws snapping behind him. He almost tripped and fell as he reached the ring of trees.

He entered the clearing and picked up one of the glowing rocks in each hand. It was the closest thing he had to a weapon. He stood there, thinking his time on the earth may be about to end. The creature slowly entered the clearing. The glowing stones revealed a large head covered in scales. Aramis immediately recognized what it was.

A phiebus.

Dangerous creatures, they were distantly related to dragons. They resembled lizards but were massively larger. The one staring at him now was huge. He guessed it to be the size of a horse. Its scales were diamond-shaped and as black as the shadows of the shrine. He had seen only two in his lifetime. One from a distance as a boy. The other he had hunted with his father. Supposedly the species was on the brink of extinction, and for good reason.

Aramis felt as though his heart were pounding in his head. When his father and he had hunted one, they had several soldiers to help them and narrowly avoided being killed. Aramis knew he was overmatched. He stepped back as the phiebus lowered its head. The scales of the creature's neck began to glow red. Aramis turned and threw himself to the ground as a blast of fire exploded through the clearing.

He scrambled to his feet and ran as fast as his legs would go, still clutching the stones in his hand. The creature followed him, hissing and snapping. Aramis turned and threw one of the stones. It smacked the phiebus in the nose and only seemed to anger the creature further. No wonder they had not seen any priests or guards. The creature alone could handle almost any intruder.

He ran toward the gates. In the back of his mind, he knew he wasn't going to make it. The phiebus would catch him and maul him to death. He could make out Mel, his armor glinted in the moonlight, and saw he was busy fighting off several figures. Mel wouldn't be able to help him either since he couldn't enter the shrine.

Aramis tripped on some roots and fell face first. His head hit the ground hard and he lay gasping for breath. The phiebus was on him quick, clawing and biting. As soon as he gained his breath back, he rolled onto his back and slammed the glowing stone into the creature's head repeatedly. It didn't even seem to faze it.

The phiebus tried to bite his hand which caused him to drop the stone. He cursed and tried to get out from under the creature. It slammed a clawed foot onto his chest, pinning him down. He fought to free himself, but the creature was incredibly strong.

His mind raced frantically, trying to figure out how he could escape. The phiebus watched him squirming and he realized the creature was toying with him. He raised his leg and kneed the beast in the stomach. He may as well have tapped it on the shoulder for all it accomplished. Something fell beside him. He moved his head, trying to see past the phiebus's claws. The dagger the old blind woman had given him. It lay in the dirt, having fallen out of his belt.

Aramis hadn't even considered the small blade. It certainly wasn't long enough to pierce the creature's thick scales. What other option did he have? He struggled to reach the dagger with his right arm. An odd sound drew his attention to the beast's neck. It began to glow red again. Apparently, it was bored with him.

He felt the wooden hilt of the dagger with his fingertips. Stretching his arm out as far as he could, he grabbed the dagger and stabbed it toward himself, striking the phiebus's claw that had him pinned. A blinding white light flared to life. He closed his eyes and turned his head away, but his vision had already been seared. The weight of the claw lifted off of him. His eyes were watering so much he almost couldn't open them.

The phiebus had backed away, hissing and scratching at the ground. Aramis got back onto his feet. The powerful glow was coming from the blade of the dagger. He shielded his eyes and picked it up from the ground, having dropped it when the light burst forth. The phiebus continued hissing at him as it backed away. He didn't have time to wonder about the blade. He could hear the sounds of fighting still raging at the gate and knew he had to help Mel.

Turning his back to the creature, he was about to head to the gates when he heard the phiebus coming back at him. He turned around, holding the blade out as if to ward off the beast. It stopped, dropped its head, and bellowed out a breath of fire. It took him by surprise and he braced himself as the blast of fire enveloped him.

Only he didn't feel the heat. Nor did he smell smoke. The flames sputtered and died as they reached him, fading out of existence. The beast hissed and leaped through the air, landing in front of him. It stared down at him menacingly and opened its mouth again. Aramis looked at the glow coming from its neck. The reddish light illuminated a small spot where one of its scales was chipped, leaving the skin exposed.

Without thinking twice, Aramis took the opening. He

lunged forward and thrust the dagger into the beast's neck. Fire spewed out of the wound, igniting the dry grass and leaves on the ground. He yanked the blade free and staggered back. It looked like liquid fire was pouring from the phiebus's neck, burning everything it touched. The beast roared in pain, piercing the air with a high-pitched shriek. Aramis clapped his hands over his ears. It was so loud!

The fire began to burn the creature itself. The thick black scales melted from the heat. The phiebus walked forward sluggishly before slumping onto the ground. Shouts drew his attention back to the gates. He sprinted that way, feeling his belt to make sure he still had the wineskin of blood. It was there, though the cap had come loose and some of it had spilled out. He replaced the cap as he ran, but kept the dagger out.

Reaching the gates, he pulled them open and stepped out. Mel's back was to him and he was fighting an orc. An orc! Aramis thought his father's patrols had killed them all or driven them off after the battle outside Palindrom when Orlek had been defeated. He saw three bodies on the ground, all orcs. Apparently, they hadn't all been driven off. Mel swept his blade out in an arc, pushing the orc back.

He seemed to have everything handled. Aramis saw torches in the distance heading their way. "We've got company!" he yelled. Mel didn't acknowledge him other than to quickly dispatch the orc, severing its head from its body.

He turned to Aramis, running a hand through his hair and wiping sweat from his brow. "These were just scouts," he said, waving at the bodies. "They tried to go into the shrine."

"I thought only those with the mark of Mordum could enter?" Aramis asked.

Mel knelt down beside one of the bodies and lifted

the orc's arm up. He pointed. Aramis had to get closer and lean in to see. A black cross, just like the one on his own arm. "So they've aligned themselves with Mordum? That doesn't make any sense. Orcs worship their chiefs as gods."

"Cut the head off a snake, does it not still move?" Mel asked.

Aramis nodded in agreement. "They're getting closer. We've got to get out of here."

Mel pointed to the wineskin at his belt. "Is that the blood?" Aramis nodded. "What happened to you? Are you all right, my Prince? You've got blood on you." Aramis gingerly rubbed the scratches from the phiebus. Though they had stopped bleeding, they were still painful.

"There was a phiebus guarding the shrine."

"Nasty creatures," Mel said, shaking his head. "I'm surprised you survived to tell the tale." He motioned to the east. "Down the mountain," he said. Aramis didn't argue. He wanted to get as far away from this place as he could. He wasn't sure if it was the scratches or the cross, but his left arm was burning intensely. They trotted off at a jog. Aramis kept looking over his shoulder to see if the orcs had picked up their trail. It didn't appear that they had.

After an hour, they reached a flat area where they stopped to rest. "Climbing down the mountain is much easier than going up," Aramis said as he leaned against a boulder. He accepted a canteen from Mel and drank deeply. Mel sighed as he looked out over the landscape.

"What is it?" Aramis asked.

"To think that I bathed in lavender before we left, only to be covered in sweat and orc blood. It's utterly depressing."

Aramis laughed at the absurdity of that. "You're ridiculous." He took another drink and passed the canteen back to Mel. Some rocks clattered down the mountain from above. Both of them turned and looked.

"There," Mel pointed. An orc.

"They did follow us," Aramis groaned. "I don't think we can make it down the mountain without engaging them." Mel remained silent, watching as more orcs appeared above them. Another figure joined them, standing much shorter than the orcs. "Is that a man?"

"I think so," Mel answered. "I can't be sure from this distance. If it is a man, it's surely one of Mordum's priests. They were probably coming to collect the blood. We need to keep moving."

They continued downward, treading carefully so they didn't cause a rock slide or trip on anything. They didn't stop again. They couldn't afford to, not with the orcs closing in on them. After several hours, they had almost reached the bottom of the mountain. The sun was beginning to rise on the horizon, bathing the sky in brilliant reds and oranges.

Aramis looked back to see how far the orcs were. They were closing the gap. With the sun coming up, Aramis was able to more clearly see their features. They were tall and muscular, with varied skin colors. Some of them were gray skinned, but most of them had a pale green hue to their flesh. They wore steel breastplates covered in spikes and tattered clothing underneath. They wielded large battle axes and hammers. Jutting up from their lower lips were two large canines, roughly three or four inches in length.

The shorter figure kept pace with them which surprised Aramis. Orcs were stronger and faster than men, usually being able to travel three times the distance in the same amount of time. Mel tapped him on the shoulder to get his attention and handed him a small spyglass. Aramis took it and looked at the orcs through it. He counted at least fifteen. Then he looked toward the man. It *was* a man. And Aramis recognized him.

He lowered the spyglass and clenched his jaw.

"My Lord? What is it?"

Aramis stared hatefully up the mountain in silence. His breathing intensified. He would have crushed the spyglass in his grip if it weren't made of metal and glass.

"The short one up there," he said.

"That's my father's killer."

"Avoid wicked deeds like a plague."

—Precept of Zevea

CHAPTER 10

"You are certain?" Mel asked. He took the spyglass from Aramis and looked through it himself. Aramis nodded stiffly. "I'd recognize his face anywhere. I'm going to kill him." He stepped forward as if he would fulfill that pledge then and there.

Mel gripped his arm. "This isn't the place or the time," he said softly. "I know your pain, my Lord. I do. But you'd go up against orcs and a priest of Mordum with nothing but a dagger?"

Aramis stared up the mountain for a moment longer and then turned to his friend. "You are right. I cannot allow my hatred to cloud my judgment. But I *will* have my revenge." Aramis pointed at the man and glared. He didn't know if the man could see the action or not, but he swore he heard laughter echoing down behind him as they continued their trek.

They climbed over rocks and stepped over fallen trees. It was difficult trying to move quickly without tumbling down to their deaths. The orcs were getting closer. Aramis thought he could hear their heavy breathing.

"We need a new plan," Mel said between labored breaths. "We can stand and fight, but they have the high ground to their advantage. We might reach the bottom, but they'll be able to outrun us on the flat ground."

Aramis didn't have any ideas. He was struggling just to keep his pace. Fighting certainly wasn't an option; he didn't have a suitable weapon.

They walked around a massive boulder and Aramis paused. "We've got to keep moving," Mel said. Aramis looked at the boulder, then down the mountain.

"I'm getting an idea now. We can hide here and wait until they pass us. Once they do, we can push this rock down and crush them."

Mel wiped sweat from his forehead with the back of his hand. "What if it misses them? Or if they realize it's a ruse?"

"Do you have a better plan?"

Mel looked up the mountain at the approaching horde. "No. But we'll need to make sure they are in the rock's path. I'll continue down further and draw their attention. You push the rock down."

Aramis was shaking his head before Mel finished speaking. "You could also be caught in its path. And I can't push this rock myself. It's got to weigh at least a thousand pounds. I'll need your help to do this."

Mel held out his hand and summoned his sword. The silver blade materialized from mist, glinting in the light of the morning. He began cutting away at the bottom of the enormous rock, causing its balance to become precarious.

"That should be enough for you to easily push it yourself. I'm going to draw them down into its path. It's too risky for you to do it. I'm much more protected."

"You think your armor can keep you alive through an avalanche?"

Mel summoned his armor and pulled the face plate of his helm down. "Only one way to find out," he said. Before Aramis could argue further, Mel leaped away, jogging down the rocky landscape. Aramis knelt down to the right of the boulder, waiting for the orcs to pass. He counted them silently as they ran down towards Mel, who stood in a battle stance awaiting them.

The black-robed priest jogged past, taking up the rear position of the line. As soon as he passed, Aramis scrambled uphill to the backside of the boulder. He placed his hands on the rock and pushed as hard as he could. It didn't budge. He growled in frustration and pushed again. The dirt beneath his feet shifted and he had to make a walking motion to keep traction. Despite the fact that Mel had cut away most of the rock that held the boulder in place, it remained solidly stuck.

Aramis stepped back and kicked the boulder. He also threw himself bodily against it, possibly bruising his shoulder. He was sweating from the exertion. Clanging metal filled the air and he knew the orcs had engaged Mel. He had to find a way to move the rock and quickly. He turned to place his back against the rock and saw the priest standing there.

Aramis's eyes widened and he reached for the dagger at his belt. The priest spoke a word and Aramis was bound in place, unable to move. His muscles strained against an invisible force.

"You have something that belongs to me," the assassin's voice said. He stepped close to Aramis and took the wineskin filled with blood from his belt. "You also killed Mordum's pet. He is not pleased with you. The quicker you let the mark consume you, the easier your life will become."

Aramis tried to speak but nothing came out. He could

still breathe, but his vocal cords obeyed him as well as his muscles did; not at all. The priest pulled his hood back and Aramis was greeted by the familiar face of the man who murdered his father. His vision hazed as his rage boiled over. Despite his raw emotions, he still couldn't break free of the spell. He vaguely heard the sounds of fighting. Mel needed his help and yet he was useless.

"The new king is searching for you. He will kill you when he finds you. I wonder how angry he would be if I took that joy from him?" The priest continued talking, seemingly more to himself than to Aramis. "We serve the same god, but we all have different interests, you see?" He tapped his chin as if contemplating something. "I shall not kill you yet. But I will kill your friend."

The priest placed his foot on the boulder and pushed. The rock went rolling. He made it seem so easy. Then he physically turned Aramis around. It went tumbling wildly down the hill, bouncing and causing a landslide. Aramis watched in mute horror, hoping Mel would be able to escape. The massive rock crushed everything in its path. After a few minutes, the dust settled and Aramis could only see the mangled bodies of orcs. He couldn't see Mel; hopefully, that was a good sign.

Without saying anything else, the priest continued walking down the mountain. Aramis remained paralyzed until he could no longer see the priest in the distance. As the spell wore off, his muscles began to ache. He slumped down onto his knees, his entire body shaking. How could anyone stand against a man who could stop you with a single word? After a few minutes, Aramis stood back up and slowly made his way toward the bodies. He had to know.

Many of the orcs were nothing more than bloodied lumps. He had to look away lest he vomit. There was no sign of Mel. He searched all around the devastation left behind from the avalanche. He was ready to give up his search when something shiny caught his eye. It was sticking up from some loose dirt. He knelt down and realized it was a hand. Well, it was a gauntlet. Aramis grabbed it and pulled.

The dirt fell away to reveal the armored body of Mel. "Thank the gods," Aramis breathed. He paused. Did he really just say that? Pushing the thought away, he pulled Mel's faceplate up. His eyes were closed, and his skin was covered in sweat, but he seemed all right. "Mel? Mel, can you hear me?"

A long, low groan was Mel's reply. Aramis sighed in relief. "Can you move? I can help you up, but I don't want to move you in case something is broken."

Mel's eyelids blinked rapidly multiple times before they finally opened fully. He met Aramis's gaze and said, "The only thing that's broken is your sense of style."

Aramis laughed. "You're a fool, you know that? I'm surprised your armor held up to that."

Mel forced himself up out of the dirt and got to his feet. He surveyed the area, nodding to himself. "You did it," he said. "You crushed them with the boulder. What about the priest?"

"I didn't push the rock. I couldn't. It was too heavy for me. The priest pushed it down after he took the blood." Mel looked to Aramis's belt. "He cast a spell on me, I think. I couldn't move or speak. All I could do was watch." Aramis shook his head forlornly. "He's taken the blood and he's gone to who knows where. What do we do now?"

"We find him," Mel said resolutely. "We find him and we take it back." One of the orcs stirred and Aramis drew his dagger instinctively. Mel shook his head. "Leave him. We should get moving. We've got to find his trail."

Aramis hesitated, finding it odd that Mel didn't want him to kill the creature. He sheathed the dagger back at his belt. "Let's be off," he said.

Mel dismissed his armor and they made their way down the rest of the mountain. With no one pursuing them, they were able to travel at a slower pace and reserve their strength. After an hour, they reached the main road that wound its way through Oakvalor.

"It's unlikely we'll pass anyone this close to the mountains," Mel said as they walked. Aramis nodded in silence. At least the road was paved and relatively flat. His legs were still burning from the descent of the mountain. The scratches on his arm were itchy, but he tried to ignore it. The blood had dried and wasn't dripping down his arm anymore. Now that he thought about it, his hand didn't hurt.

He held his broken hand up and made a fist. Then he wiggled his fingers. He started laughing and Mel looked at him quizzically. "My hand," Aramis said. "It's not broken anymore. I hadn't realized it in all the chaos. Did you heal me?"

Mel shook his head, frowning. "It's the mark. As time goes by, other things will begin to happen."

"Like what?" Aramis asked, still flexing his hand.

"I've read it's different for everyone. Some people gain powers, others go insane. Mordum is a cruel god and shows favor to few. Let us hope we don't have to find out what it will do to you."

"The priest must have some serious power. I struggled to push that boulder and couldn't do it. It seemed like he moved it without much effort. And his eyes looked strange."

Mel stopped walking. He tilted his head. "What do you mean? What about his eyes were strange?"

"They were black," Aramis answered.

"A templar," Mel said softly. Aramis didn't hear him.

"A what?"

"A templar," he repeated. "They are the elite of Mordum's forces. I've never encountered one before, but I have heard stories. The Prophet battled one a few years ago. He managed to kill the templar, but it wasn't easy. They are said to be gifted with many dark powers and are almost impossible to defeat. The Prophet only managed it by the power of Edria."

Aramis took it all in. He would still get his revenge. Given this new information, he wasn't sure how, but that wasn't going to deter him.

"Brookhaven is the nearest town," Mel said, changing the subject. "We should make it there by nightfall. We can eat and get some rest. Then we can decide what to do in the morning." Aramis voiced his agreement with the plan and they continued walking.

When they finally reached the town, the sun was just setting. Aramis found the place welcoming. Children ran through the streets, heading home for dinner after a long day of playing. People were closing down their shops. The only places that seemed to stay open were the inns and a single bar. The only difference between the two was the bar didn't have rooms to rent.

They rented a room from the only inn that had a vacancy. Mel insisted they go to the bathhouse to wash up before getting anything to eat. Aramis was so exhausted the only thing he wanted to do was sleep. He was too tired to argue with Mel, so they ended up at the bath house. Sitting in the hot water relaxed his muscles and Aramis had to concede that Mel's idea had been a good one.

As they bathed, the attendants took their clothes and washed them. Though he was still sore, Aramis felt refreshed after the bath. The attendants also bandaged their wounds and scrapes for them after applying a healing salve. He almost felt like he was back at the castle.

It reminded him that he had a duty to his people. They couldn't remain leaderless. The petty nobles would plunge the kingdom into civil war, similar to Talvaard's current state. He also kept thinking about what the blind woman and the templar had said. A "new" king. Had someone usurped the throne? What kind of chaos was the castle in? There were so many things he didn't know.

Aramis went back to the inn and claimed one of the empty tables. He didn't think it was likely anyone would recognize him this far from the capital, so he didn't bother to conceal himself. The barmaid came to take his order, but as hungry as he was he wanted to wait for Mel. After thirty minutes of waiting, he was about to get up and go looking for his friend when Mel walked into the inn.

He was smiling as he made his way over to the table. "It's about time," Aramis said.

"I'm sorry for the delay, my Lord. I was enjoying an amazingly talented woman's hands."

Aramis raised his brow quizzically. Mel's face flushed in embarrassment. "I should clarify I meant a massage. I was enjoying a massage. Took the pain right out of my neck."

"I'm starving," Aramis said, "and you are getting your back rubbed? I could have eaten and gone to bed already."

Mel's eyes widened. "I'm sorry! If I'd have known you were waiting on me to eat, I'd have skipped the massage until after our meal." Mel waved the barmaid over and they ordered some food and wine. It didn't take long for her to bring their order. As they ate, Aramis noticed that Mel kept looking at the door every time someone entered the inn.

"Waiting on someone?" Aramis asked curiously.

"I'm merely being cautious," Mel answered. "We

can't talk about it here, but I learned some interesting things from the bathhouse girl." They finished their meal and Mel led Aramis outside, much to his displeasure. He just wanted to get some sleep. They walked to the edge of the town before Mel would answer any of his questions. Even then, Mel kept a close watch at any passerby with an intensity that probably made the strangers uncomfortable.

"Mel, I'm exhausted. Please get on with it already." Aramis stood with his arms folded.

"I'm sorry, my Lord. I have to be sure we aren't being watched. The girl seemed a little too open about what she knew. It appears the priest of Mordum came through here not too long before us." That piqued Aramis's interest. He tilted his head and waited for Mel to continue.

"He scared several of the townspeople pretty well. He came through long enough to eat, without paying, and left. The town guard seemed to know who he was because they were too frightened to approach him about the unpaid bill. When I asked the girl if anyone knew which direction he headed, she said the local blacksmith saw him go west, riding off on a horse the likes of which he'd never seen before."

"Is that it? You snuck around and looked at everyone as if they were a criminal over that bit of information?" Aramis shook his head.

"As I said, I was being careful. She was very willing to talk about the priest despite the guards being afraid of him. She could be a spy."

That could be true, but Aramis doubted it. "So he went back the way we came from? We didn't pass anyone on the road. The Viss Mountains stretch the entire border of my kingdom all the way to the Deadlands. He couldn't have ridden a horse—" Aramis cut off his words, remembering how the priest had climbed the walls of the castle.

Mel nodded, probably thinking the same thing. "So he headed where? To Talvaard? Why would he go west?" Aramis asked.

Mel shrugged. "I've been pondering the same thing. I will send word to the Prophet and see what information he can provide."

"How are you going to do that? We don't have time to wait for a courier to go to Kaldore and back."

"Edria has given us other means of communication," Mel replied. "We can communicate through prayer. We don't do it often, as it is taxing on our strength. I will pray before we retire so I will have time to rejuvenate. It bothers me that he went west. Aside from another follower of Mordum being in Talvaard, I cannot discern why he would head that way. There is constant division in Mordum's ranks, so I don't believe they are working together. There is only one way to find out," Mel said.

Aramis unfolded his arms and rubbed his face. "We must travel to Talvaard," he said, groaning inwardly.

"Precisely," Mel answered.

● ∞ ● ∞ ●

After they returned to the inn, Aramis went to his room to get some much-needed sleep. Mel went to his own room, deeply troubled by the events of the day. Kneeling before the bed, he withdrew a medallion from under his shirt.

Holding it in his hands, he focused his mind and reached out through Edria's connection. He waited only a moment before he heard the Prophet's words in his mind.

Melchiades, he greeted, *I trust all is well?*

I wish it were so, Mel answered. *We have crossed paths with a templar. He could have killed us both easily, but he spared Aramis. He may believe he killed me, but Edria's blessed armor kept me safe. Aramis was able to retrieve the blood, but the Templar took it. According to people in the town we are in, he headed west. What is in the west that would send him that way?*

There was a pause. *There are rumors that Mordum has an outpost somewhere on the edge of Talvaard. None of our agents have been able to find the place if the rumor holds true. What of the prince's progression? Has the mark begun to take over his mind?*

Not that I have seen, Mel said. *He appears to be holding it off. He is strong of mind. I don't think the mark will take him easily. The faster we can retrieve the blood, the faster we can get him back to you. I do hope you can find a way to remove the mark. Have you found anything yet?*

Melchiades, listen carefully to my instruction. Edria has abandoned the prince. He bears the mark of Mordum. Our goddess refuses to aid him in any way. Let him help you retrieve the blood and then wash your hands of the man. That is the will of Edria.

Mel was taken aback, so much so that he almost lost the connection. He shook his head in disbelief. *What are you saying? Edria would never abandon someone in need. Are you sure you heard her correctly? Surely this is not the will of the goddess!*

Calm yourself, the Prophet said, *You allow your emotions to cloud your mind. One man is not worth the cost of the world. We do what is right and true for the sake of humanity. Perhaps I should have assigned another to watch over the prince. Your friendship with him is hindering your ability to obey Edria. Do as I have commanded and return to Kaldore in haste.*

The connection severed. Mel opened his eyes and put the medallion back. He trusted the Prophet above any man, but this did not seem right. It twisted his gut and made him feel ill. He numbly climbed into the bed and lay on his back, staring up at the ceiling. He silently pleaded to Edria, asking her to help Aramis.

He eventually fell asleep, hoping Edria had heard his prayers.

"Kings will fall and cities will burn."

—Tairu

CHAPTER 11

It was hard to breathe.

Jovanna *forced* breath into her lungs. Her ears were ringing loudly, but at least the magic wasn't pounding at her anymore. She continued to lay there until she could somewhat breathe again. She got up slowly. She was surprised to see several elves up and moving. She thought for sure they had all died. As she looked around, she saw that many of Velent's warriors *had* died.

Gruesomely, some of the elves had been blown apart completely and their limbs lay far from their bodies. There was nothing left of the elf who had been glowing. She walked over to the group of elves who had survived. Of Velent's fifty men, only half had survived. And some of them probably wouldn't be able to walk. She hoped her illusion had endured the magical blast.

She noticed the elf who had been talking her ear off the entire march was among the group. He nodded toward her as she joined them. She nodded back. One of the elves was tending a wound on Velent's arm. He was yelling at everyone, but Jovanna didn't know if it was from the blast or out of anger. He glanced at her when she walked up but turned his attention back to the elf he was yelling at. Apparently, her illusion was still up.

A horn sounded in the distance. Everyone turned toward the direction it sounded from and drew their weapons. Jovanna reached to her belt and grabbed air. She looked down and remembered she had been carrying her sword when she was flung to the ground. She spotted her sword in the sand close to where she fell. She retrieved it and rejoined the elves.

She could make out a large force in the distance. Most likely it was their enemy coming to meet them. Velent began giving orders and directing his men to take positions in hiding. They were going to try and ambush the enemy. Jovanna hid on the backside of one of the huts, out of view from the road. And then they waited.

Roughly twenty minutes later, the enemy entered the village. Jovanna counted at least a hundred warriors. A few of them had skin color different than the others. She thought it odd that she had never seen that before, but she had only been among Velent's tribesmen. She scoured their ranks, hoping to find their mysterious leader among them, but she didn't see him. She did see the elder who had run away. Part of him, anyway. His head was impaled upon a wooden shaft and carried at the head of the army.

A whistle sounded; Velent's signal. She waited a moment and watched as chaos unfolded among the enemy warriors. Velent's men had surprised them. She joined in the fray, cutting down several elves quickly. They were no match for her skill with the blade. She risked a glance at Velent and saw him fighting ferociously despite the wound to his arm.

The initial shock had worn off and the enemy warriors formed into small organized groups. Velent's men had managed to take down a third of the warriors, but now they were hard pressed. They were still highly outnumbered. Two elves came at Jovanna. She leaped backward out of their reach and swung her sword horizontally. She missed and one of them charged her. He landed a solid punch to the left side of her face and she staggered back.

She growled in anger and spun her blade out in front of her in a weaving pattern. She was quicker than he was, and she managed to push him back and put him on the defensive. The other elf was one that had a different skin color. He stepped out in front of her, putting his body in the path of her blade. She smirked as she put more strength behind the swing.

The blade smacked into him and bounced off, leaving her hands throbbing. She managed to keep her grip on the blade and was surprised to see him still standing. Her surprise escalated when she realized her blade had not even nicked his flesh. He came at her, swinging an elven pole-sword at her. It was a primitive weapon, consisting of a wooden staff with a six-inch blade on each end.

She easily deflected his move. He grabbed the weapon in both hands and was pulling it back toward himself. Stepping forward, she brought her sword up and over in an overhanded chopping motion and sliced the wooden staff in two. Unfazed, the elf wielded each piece like two swords. Jovanna saw an opening and thrust her sword forward, attempting to hit him in the stomach. Again the blade bounced off his skin with nothing to show for it.

Backing away, she watched him intently, trying to discern what kind of magic was keeping her sword at bay. She didn't sense any spells other than his tattoo magic. She wondered if it was possible that a tattoo could produce such a strong spell. She didn't know much about the elven tattoo magic; they were very secretive about it. She also couldn't figure out a way around the spell. It was as though his skin had been transformed into a layer or rock.

She remembered then that the elder who ran away had said something about "stone-skin". She needed to find out what it was. She spun around and threw her leg out, slamming it into the elf's ankles and knocking him from his feet. Before he could get back up, she jumped over him and cut down the other elf. Then she jogged over to a group of Velent's warriors and took up a position next to them.

The elf who had marched in front of her was in the group as well. He moved to stand beside her. "Stone-skin," he said, motioning to the elf she had knocked down. He was back on his feet. She looked at him and shrugged.

"You must be mute."

She nodded. That would keep her from having to speak.

"Stone-skin is a tattoo our people used to use when we fought against the humans. Some of the elders said that the knowledge of this tattoo was lost, but somebody has found it. They think it is the Uniter."

Jovanna scoffed. They came up with names and titles for everything.

"It's a dangerous tattoo to get. It doesn't work on everyone. Either it makes the skin change, or you die. The elders believe this is what happened to the elf we found. His body rejected the tattoo and it destroyed him."

Jovanna stared at the elf with the stone skin. How could she counter the tattoo if it was in his skin, and his skin was now as hard as stone? She wouldn't be able to cut it. She wished her illusion could mask her voice so that she could ask questions. She would have to make due.

She stared at the magic that floated through the air.

The particles swirled around the elf, like miniature flashing lights. Why were they doing that? As she continued to stare, she noticed that while the magic was swirling around him, some of the lights were disappearing. It looked as if his body, or more specifically his tattoo, was siphoning the magic.

She watched a few moments longer. That's exactly what his tattoo was doing. She looked to the elf standing beside her and grinned, then ran out to battle the elf again. He didn't say anything to stop her. They charged each other and she used her sword to deflect his two blades. She needed to get close; dangerously close. She dipped down under one of his swings and spun up behind him. She lifted her leg and kicked him hard in the back, flinging him forward.

To his credit, he didn't fall. She growled and closed the distance. He turned to face her and she managed to knock one of the blades from his grasp. She switched her blade to her left hand and locked her sword against his remaining blade. Then she held her right hand above the tattoo that was sucking in the magic. She focused on the swirling lights and commanded them to obey her.

The tattoo was strong, but her will was stronger. The magic stopped flowing into him. His body stiffened and his jaw clenched. She balled her hand into a fist and "pulled" the magic away from him. He gasped aloud and dropped to one knee. She kept her concentration, willing the magic to keep away from him. And it obeyed.

The color of his skin began to change to a normal hue. She knew the change had to be painful because he kept grunting and crying out. When she felt his skin had become normal enough, she released her control on the magic. Gripping her sword in both hands, she spun a complete circle and easily lopped off his head. Blood splattered and the head thudded into the dirt.

A cheer rang out from Velent's warriors. Jovanna

raised her sword in the air and bellowed a war cry. Then she charged the nearest group of enemies, cutting through their midst with abandon. Velent's warriors followed her example, and though they were outnumbered, they fought more fiercely than their enemy. Jovanna took down another stone skin elf similar to the way she handled the first. It seemed to have put the fear in them as Jovanna heard the elves call for a retreat with their horns.

Velent's warriors let out another cheer and started to pursue the enemy before Velent ordered them to stay put. He told his warriors to burn the dead and assemble themselves at the edge of the village. Then he stalked over to Jovanna and stopped in front of her, staring intently into her eyes.

"I declined your request to fight with us. So tell me, why are you here?" He glared at her. She assumed he realized who she was by her spellcasting. Elves only used tattoo magic.

"I'm here because I want to avenge Jerik. Stop wasting my time with questions to which you already know the answer."

"You disobey me and then you mock me? I should have you put to death."

She laughed. "Try it. I dare you." She tightened her grip on the hilt of her sword. "If it wasn't for me, you'd have lost this battle. You've lost half your warriors as it is. You can't deny you need my blade. Not without sounding like a foolish brat."

"You'd have me look like a weak leader by allowing a woman, a *human* woman no less, to fight with our men?" He spat on the ground at her feet.

"I can keep this illusion for weeks, *elf*. And I don't need your permission to fight my own enemies."

They locked stares. Finally, Velent cursed and stormed away. Jovanna watched him go, knowing she had beaten him. Now that she knew how to kill the elves with stone skin, Velent would need her too much to send her away. She had pushed him into a precarious position. Despite their hatred for one another, she knew he was a good leader when it came to battle. At least he had that in his favor.

She knelt down next to the elf she had decapitated. His skin had completely turned back to its normal color. She examined the body, making note of tattoos she had never seen before. There were at least a dozen of them. The tattoo that had given the elf stone skin appeared to be made from a different type of ink, as well.

A puddle of blood had formed at the neck where his head had once been. Jovanna stared at it, reminded of a time long ago. She turned her attention back to the tattoos. She would need to study these new ones. One could not defend against an enemy if one did not know about their strengths. She used her sword to cut the elf's skin off, rubbed it in the dirt to dry the blood, then rolled the skin up and tucked it into her boot.

She stood up and surveyed the rest of the carnage. Bodies of the enemy tribe littered the abandoned village. She smiled at the death around her.

It had been a good day so far.

—Jovanna

CHAPTER 12

Fourteen Years Ago

She was turning six.

Normally her parents would get her a small frosted muffin from the local bakery and present it to her on her birthday. Her mother would sing her a song that her mother had sang to her when she was a child, and her father would give her a speech about the importance of getting older and learning something that would make her a valuable member of the community.

Jovanna's father was a farmer. They had the largest field of wheat in the region. Her father didn't make enough to be wealthy, but they never went hungry either. Her mother helped with the planting in the early spring, but she normally spent her time sewing clothing that would be sent to the castle for the nobles. Since the styles in the court seemed to change as often as the weather, her mother had a steady stream of work to keep her busy.

Their house was small compared to the other farmers' homes, but her father had made sure to have a sewing room so her mother could work from their home and not have to travel into town for work. Her mother would get up with the sunrise and sew for hours, stopping long enough to make lunch and then sewing until it was time to prepare dinner.

Her father would come home dirty and tired, but always smiling. He would greet her mother first, giving her a gentle kiss and then sweep Jovanna up into the air and tell her about the latest snake or gopher or other creature that he had killed in the fields. He would clean up and then they would eat dinner as a family.

That's how most days went. Sometimes her father would come home drunk, and she didn't like to think about those times. Her birthdays were always different. Her father would skip working the fields and take her to town, letting her peruse the new items in the shops and buying her one thing that she liked most.

When they returned home, her mother would have spent the day sewing her a new dress or a fancy looking shirt. She would eat the frosted muffin and go to bed feeling like the most important person in the world. She looked forward to her birthday every year for those reasons. And her birthday was always like that. At least, they were. This one would be much different.

Jovanna stared out the window of the orphanage, watching the other children play outside. She sighed and began pacing around the room, counting her steps. She walked from the window to the door and counted sixty steps, then walked from wall to wall and lost count twice before counting one hundred and twenty steps. She did this several times every day, usually getting the same numbers. Sometimes a few of the other kids would ask her to come outside with them, but she ignored them.

She didn't like other kids. In fact, she didn't like

other people. They all treated her differently like she was some kind of oddity. It was probably because of what happened to her parents. It didn't matter to her what they thought. What happened had happened and there was nothing that could change it. Was she upset? Of course. But if she had learned anything in her six short years it was that being upset didn't change anything.

When she first arrived at the orphanage, one of the other children asked her what brought her there. She tried explaining the events that led to her arrival, but the girl screamed and ran from the room before she could finish. Then she was scolded later by one of the adults for telling lies and trying to scare other children.

Jovanna shook as her head as she thought about it. She wished it were all lies. She wished it were all some story she had read in a book and not the reality of her life. Her mother always told her, "If you don't like how life is going, then change it." And that's exactly what Jovanna was going to do.

She was going to run away from the orphanage.

It had only been a couple of months, but she couldn't stand it any longer. There were too many kids crammed into the room. There weren't even enough beds for everyone. Not that Jovanna cared about that so much. She just *really* didn't like people. And here in the orphanage, she was surrounded by them. She loved the open fields of her family's wheat farm. She enjoyed the company of the wildlife and the floating white lights that seemed drawn to her.

She still saw the lights, even as she paced the room, but it wasn't the same. It hadn't been the same since …

She stopped pacing as she noticed one of the other children standing in the doorway staring at her.

"Do you want to come outside?" the girl asked.

Jovanna ignored her and began pacing the room again. The girl didn't leave. Usually, when she ignored them, they would leave. After a few minutes of watching Jovanna pacing back and forth, the girl began doing the same thing.

Jovanna stopped. "What are you doing?" she demanded.

The girl stopped as well. "I'm counting. That's what you are doing, right? I can tell by the way you are walking around that you are counting your steps. It's sixty-two steps from the window to the door and one hundred and eighteen from that wall to this one."

Jovanna just stared at her.

"I know because I counted them when I first got here. My village was burned down by some thieves and my parents didn't make it out of the house in time. What happened to your parents?"

"I don't want to talk about it," Jovanna said. She started pacing again. The girl copied her.

"It helps, you know. Talking about it. I still cry sometimes because I miss them, but talking about them helps."

"I killed them," Jovanna said. "Is that what you want me to say? I killed them and they are never coming back. And no, it doesn't help me to talk about it. Nothing helps except the lights!" She hadn't realized it, but she was yelling and had clenched her fists. The girl looked frightened. She looked like she was about to say something, but instead, she turned and fled. Jovanna gritted her teeth and walked to the window. She watched the girl run to one of the adults. The same woman who had scolded her before. The woman looked up at her.

"Great," she muttered as she turned from the window.

● ∞ ● ∞ ●

After they had eaten dinner and been sent to their

beds, Jovanna lay in the darkened room staring at the ceiling. She had it all planned out already. She would wait until everyone was asleep and then she would get up and sneak down the stairs. The orphanage didn't employ guards, so she didn't have to worry about getting past anyone.

She just had to get a key from one of the adults so she could unlock the main doors and get outside. She figured all of that would be pretty easy except for getting the key. There were five adults who helped care for all of the orphans. Jovanna had thought long and hard about which one to try and take the key from. She had finally decided to take it from the adult who had scolded her earlier.

She lay there for as long as she could bear. She got up off the floor. She considered taking the blanket with her, but she wasn't sure how she'd carry it. It was twice as long as she was and she would need to carry food. She hesitated a few more seconds and left it, heading out of the door and into the hallway. It was completely dark except for a single candle that stayed lit through the night. Jovanna blew it out as she passed.

The adult's room was downstairs next to the pantry. Jovanna took that as a sign that she had made the right choice. She would get the key, grab some food, and escape into the night. Some of the boards creaked as she walked. Each time it happened, she would pause mid-step and wait. Perhaps it seemed louder to her since she was trying to be quiet.

She reached the door and waited. Her heart was hammering in her chest. What would happen if they caught her trying to sneak out? Would they punish her? And if they did, how bad would it be? Jovanna swallowed hard and twisted the door handle, pushing it open carefully. A candle burned on the nightstand next to the adult's bed. She was propped upright on her pillows with a book in her hand. For a moment, Jovanna thought the woman was awake.

Then she noticed that the woman's eyes were closed. She shook her head, suddenly realizing the absurdity of what she was doing. She almost gave up and went back upstairs. She thought of her mother, though, and that gave her some strength. She walked slowly and quietly to the nightstand. The key was laying there, gently reflecting the candlelight. The candle rested on a small, thin metal stand. It was probably worth something.

Using her left hand, she laid it on the key and slid it across the wood. The soft scraping sound woke the woman, and she drowsily looked at Jovanna.

"What are you doing?" she asked, frowning.

Jovanna panicked. She couldn't stay in the orphanage. She hated people. She especially hated *these* people. They took her from her farmhouse and brought her to this horrible place. Dozens of scary scenarios played out in her mind. Her eyes widened as the woman sat forward, becoming more awake. "Why are you in here? Did you have a nightmare—"

Crack!

Jovanna smacked her across the face with the metal candle holder. She watched in horrid fascination as blood and hot wax splattered across the wall. The woman's body slammed back onto her pillows and she lay very still.

Dread washed over her as she realized that she had probably killed the woman. She dropped the candlestick and backed up slowly, her eyes watering up. What had she done? First her parents, and now this woman?

Turning to the door, she ran straight past the pantry and to the main doors. She struggled to get the key into the lock. Her tears were making it hard to see clearly. Finally, she managed to undo the lock. She pulled one of the doors open and stood there, suddenly terrified.

Where was she going to go? She hadn't thought that far ahead.

She heard something behind her. She didn't wait to see who it was. She ran as fast as she could. She passed through the yard where the other children played, past the houses and shops that lined the streets. She kept running, not going in any specific direction. Her mind raced. Where could she go? No one would want her. She could go to the slums. She heard that many kids lived there on their own.

Jovanna headed in that direction, her small bare feet slapping against the cobblestone road. As she got closer, she realized that if the others at the orphanage knew she killed the woman, they would come looking for her. The town guard might even come looking to apprehend her.

She stopped in the street, breathing heavily. She looked back toward the orphanage, and then to the slums. She would need to hide. Not forever, but long enough that they would stop looking for her. There was one place they wouldn't be able to find her. She changed direction and started running again.

A few minutes later she reached the place. It looked much more frightening in the dark. She gritted her teeth and tried not to be afraid. Then she ran into the place that she would now call home.

She entered the garbage dump.

"Cling dearly to the truth."

—Precept of Zevea

CHAPTER 13

Everything was gray.

Aramis looked out over a desolate landscape. Dry grass and dead trees covered the terrain. He wondered briefly where he was, and when he tried to remember how he got there, his mind went blank. He was standing on a hilltop, looking down into a small valley. And everything was shaded in a gray hue. Even the shafts of sunlight that filtered through the clouds seemed to be devoid of any real light.

From his vantage point, he saw that a stream ran through the valley to the far right. He was thirsty, and so he made his way down the hill and toward the water. He noticed a slight breeze was blowing because brittle leaves tumbled across the ground and flitted about in the air. Oddly he couldn't feel the wind at all.

As he neared the stream, he noticed that the banks were littered with fish, all dead. Some had already begun decomposing. A few were nothing more than bones. The water flowed at a gentle pace, belying whatever sinister thing that had ended the fish's lives. Aramis was much thirstier than he had first thought. His throat was parched. He gazed into the water, unsure if he should try to drink it.

"A little shouldn't hurt," he said to himself. Kneeling down, he cupped his hands and filled them with water. It was neither warm nor cold against his skin. Indeed, he couldn't even tell that the water was in his hands other than the fact that he could clearly see it was. He lifted it to his lips and took a sip. It was salty and tasted like copper. It reminded him of a time when he was younger and had put a coin into his mouth.

He opened his hands and released the water, shaking his head at the foulness. He rubbed his wet hands along his arms. The black cross started to itch. He scratched at it absent-mindedly, gazing into the water of the stream. Something about the water seemed odd, besides the nasty taste. The texture of it seemed thicker than what it should have been. His hands felt sticky. He looked at them, and though everything was gray, he could immediately tell it was not water.

It was blood.

Aramis gagged and spit to clean his mouth out. It did little to comfort his mind. He turned from the stream and his arm began to burn. He looked at the cross and saw the skin was starting to bubble up, like a pot of water that was beginning to boil. Only the bubbles didn't dissipate, they moved along his arm toward his fingers and began to drip onto the ground. They looked like circular black bugs spiraling down onto the ground.

Somewhere in the back of his mind, he knew this felt similar to something else he had seen, but he couldn't place it. The skin itched and burned like fire. He gritted his teeth against the pain. The last few bubbles of black skin dripped from his fingertips to the ground and he rubbed the painful spot on his arm where the cross had been.

The black liquid moved along the ground of its own accord, flowing into the stream and mixing with the blood. A figure took shape from the blood, rising up out of the stream and stepping onto the banks. The wind picked up, ruffling their clothes and whipping the figure's hood off his head. His face was gaunt and unnaturally pale. His head was nearly bald, with only a few wisps of hair remaining and a scraggly goatee hung down from his chin. His eyes were sunken deep into his head, the pupils devoid of color.

Despite the fact that the man seemed ready for the grave, he radiated a sinister power that made Aramis's flesh crawl. "Who are you?" he asked.

"I have many names, but you know me as Mordum." The man's lips barely moved, but his voice echoed across the landscape. With blinding quickness, Mordum was suddenly standing mere inches from him. The smell of decay assaulted Aramis and made his eyes water.

"Their blood calls to me night and day," Mordum said. "And soon I shall answer." Aramis didn't know what he was talking about. He would have asked, but he feared if he stopped holding his breath he might inhale some disease from the man.

"The faithful continue to gather. When the moon is high, and all have been gathered, I shall sweep over the earth like a plague. None can stop the coming of death!"

Mordum grabbed Aramis by the throat and held him up off the ground, choking him. Aramis struggled to break Mordum's grip, but he was too strong. Mordum's hand was intensely cold against his neck. His vision began to blur as he struggled to breathe. Then Mordum released him and he fell backward, seeing everything in slow motion. And then he hit the ground.

● ∞ ● ∞ ●

Aramis awoke, kicking and swinging. It took several moments for his mind to figure out where he was. He was lying in his bed at the inn. He was breathing heavy and covered in a thick sheen of sweat. He slumped back against the pillows and sighed in relief.

It had seemed so real to him. He didn't think it wise to try and go back to sleep, so he got up and walked over to the window. It was still dark. He wasn't sure what time it was. He grabbed his shirt from off the floor, apparently having taken it off in his sleep. He pulled it over his head, threw on his boots, and left his room. He headed down to the tavern area.

All of the chairs had been placed on top of the tables and the barmaid that had brought their food was mopping the wooden floors. Two men, drunk judging by their boisterous conversation, sat at the bar sipping from their mugs. The barmaid paused in her cleaning.

"Can I get you anything?" she asked.

Aramis shook his head. "No, thank you. I just need some fresh air."

"You're pale as chalk," she said. "Are you ill? There's a doctor at the edge of town if you need one."

Aramis tried to smile reassuringly. "I'm not sick. Just bad dreams. I'm going to step outside." She nodded and went back to mopping. He walked to an area that didn't appear to have been cleaned yet and exited through the door.

The streets were empty, which he expected at this hour. Every twenty feet or so, a lantern hung from a lamp post or off the side of a building, providing light with which to see. The sky was cloudless and Aramis figured even if there weren't lanterns, he probably would have been able to see clearly by the light of the moon.

The roads were all paved with cobblestone. Aramis's

great great grandfather was responsible for that. He had paid for all roads in Oakvalor to be paved so that trade could be improved. Some of his detractors claimed it was really done so the king could move his armies about the realm faster. Aramis knew it was actually due to the first reason.

While he preferred spending his time with the soldiers outdoors, he did study many topics at the direction of his tutors growing up. He read several biographies of people from his lineage, as well as their personal journals. He obviously never met the man, but judging by the thoughts he recorded in his journal, Aramis knew him to be a good and just ruler. Just like his father.

Tears stung his eyes at the thought of his father. He didn't hold them back. He wondered how his mother was holding up. The funeral had probably already happened, and he couldn't even attend it because he was running around the kingdom like a criminal. The young spoiled prince in him wanted to feel sorry for himself, but the growing kingly part of him knew there would be time to grieve later.

He stopped walking when he reached a darkened building that appeared to be vacant and sat down on the steps of the porch. He stared up into the sky at the moon, silently praying. And then he laughed at himself. He didn't believe in the gods, any of them, and yet here he was giving lip service to any one of them that would listen. Aramis had often debated with his religious tutor.

He was adamant that the gods did not exist. He attributed "miracles" to natural events that couldn't readily be explained. His teacher would always counter with, "If you don't believe in the gods, why do you always pray to them when you are in trouble?" He always denied that he did, but deep inside he knew his tutor hit the sword on the shield.

Why indeed?

A noise on the road ahead of him drew his attention. A familiar wooden cart came rolling into view. The blind woman he had met previously was pushing it along the street. She slowed her pace as she neared him.

"Prince Aramis," she greeted.

"Lady," he returned. He couldn't remember her name. As he thought about it, he couldn't remember her ever giving him her name. "What are you doing out this late? Granted this town seems safe enough, but aren't you afraid vagabonds might try to rob you or your goods?"

The woman cackled loudly. "I have no fear of highway robbers," she answered. "What I have cannot be stolen, only given." He doubted that, but he didn't say it. "How do you travel from place to place so fast?" he asked.

"I'm afraid I don't know what you are talking about," she laughed again. Aramis shook his head in defeat. "You talk cryptically every time I see you. I pray one day you will give me a straight answer."

"That's something you are doing more often," she said with a grin.

"Praying or wanting a straight answer?"

Her answer was another laugh. Aramis grunted and shook his head in frustration. He didn't know why he humored the crazy old woman. She hobbled around to the side of the cart facing him and leaned against it.

"Do you still have the dagger I gave you?" she asked.

"I do," he said. He didn't have it on him currently, but it was in his room at the inn.

"I assume it helped you at the right time?"

More of her confusing talk. "It hasn't. Actually—" he stopped. It had been a huge help in his fight with the phiebus back at the shrine. "How did you know?" he asked.

"Know what?"

"When you gave it to me, you said something about it being the only thing that would work. I used it to kill a phiebus. I've hunted them before with my father. The fire of their breath can easily melt steel. The dagger wasn't damaged at all." He stared at her intently. "Are you a seer?"

"Something like that," she laughed again.

"Seriously, I want to know. Who are you?"

"You are not ready for that," she said, her tone growing solemn. "But your friend is close," she added.

"Mel?" he asked.

The woman nodded. "I told you before, Aramis. Revelation will come in time."

Aramis sighed loudly. "I came out here to get some air and clear my mind. Every time I see you, I walk away with more questions than I started with. Can I ask you a question without you giving me an indirect answer?"

"I will do my best," she answered.

"You mentioned something before about a new king. Do you know if someone has usurped the throne in my absence? I obviously haven't heard much being on the run. I would appreciate anything you know."

The woman was silent for a moment. "The new king is your brother."

Aramis scoffed. "I don't have a brother. I'm the only child, excluding my dead sister."

"That you know of," she replied.

"That's ridiculous," he said, rising from the stairs. "I would know if I had a brother." He started to walk away, headed back towards the inn.

"He was banished before you were born," the woman said. Aramis paused. It sounded insane. A brother? Why would his parents have hidden this from him? It seemed unlikely. He turned to face her.

"My parents were older when they had me. I was hailed as a miracle child. Why would that be said of me if I had an older brother?"

"Who told you that your birth was miraculous?" she asked.

"Everyone," he answered.

"Your parents told you this?"

He hesitated. "Perhaps. The nobles said it constantly when I was younger."

"Why would the nobles tell you that but not your own parents? Consider that."

Aramis shook his head and turned his back to her. "I wanted a straight answer," he growled.

"I gave you one. Revelation will—"

"Come in time," he finished for her. Then he stalked angrily back to the inn. He looked over his shoulder to make sure she wasn't following him. He didn't see any sign of her or her cart. Good, he thought. The woman infuriated him. Her riddles, it seemed, had become lies.

He entered the inn to find everyone had retired. The barmaid had left a single lantern lit on one of the tables to provide enough light for him to navigate to his room. He made a mental note to thank her in the morning. He got back to his room and threw himself onto the bed. All he wanted was to clear his name and take care of the kingdom his father had worked to make a better place. Eventually, he fell into a fitful sleep.

● ∞ ● ∞ ●

The next morning, Aramis got up and performed his ablutions. When he was finished, he went to Mel's door and knocked. When no answer came, he shrugged and went down to the tavern area. He found his friend already seated at a table. Aramis joined him.

"Good morning, my Lord," Mel greeted. Aramis

nodded his head in acknowledgment and looked around the tavern. There were a few people scattered throughout, most of them eating breakfast.

"Have you ordered yet?" he asked Mel.

"I have," Mel answered. "I heard they serve some of the best potatoes in the kingdom. I ordered us both a plate with eggs and some bread. I hope that is suitable?"

Aramis nodded. "I'm starved," he said. He looked around again to make sure none of the people in the tavern were paying attention to them. He leaned across the table and lowered his voice. "I had another vision."

Mel stiffened. "Let me see your arm," he said. Aramis placed his arm on the table for his friend to inspect. Mel stared intently at the mark and finally shook his head.

"I'm not sure, but it might be a shade darker than it was. Time is always against us, it seems. We need to leave as soon as we are done eating. What happened in the vision?"

Aramis was about to answer when the barmaid delivered their food. She set two large plates down. Aramis's mouth watered at the sight of the steaming potatoes. The eggs looked just as appealing. He looked at the barmaid and smiled. "Thank you for leaving the lantern for me last night. I appreciate it."

She scrunched her face up in confusion. "I would say you are welcome, but I didn't leave a lantern out. When I left, this place was as dark as a cave. What do you want to drink?" she asked them. Mel asked for wine while Aramis ordered water. She left and returned a moment later with the drinks. She set them on the table and left to greet two men who had entered the tavern.

They both began eating. Mel made several odd sounds that Aramis took as compliments to the taste of the food. He talked as they ate, relating his dream to Mel. He also told her about how the blind woman met him on the road when he went to clear his mind.

"There's something about that woman that puts me on edge," Mel said. "She knows too much to be blind."

Aramis nodded in agreement. "I know. You saw what I saw, though. Her eyes are missing from her head. I think she is a seer. I read about them in my studies. Some of them don't need eyes to see. They have some kind of power that produces images of their surroundings in their minds. I asked her if she was one, and she said 'something like that'."

Mel tapped the table with his finger. "That could explain it."

Aramis ate the last bit of food on his place and pushed it to the center of the table. Mel had already finished his and they both stood up. Mel placed a few coins on the table and they left the tavern.

"I tried to get some horses, but none of the stables had any that could make it up the mountain. We'll have to go on foot until we get to Talvaard."

"Can our luck get any worse?" Aramis asked.

"I'm sure it's about to," Mel replied.

"Why do you say that?"

"Because we're being followed."

"Do not say you know a man until you have fought beside him."

—Prince Aramis

CHAPTER 14

The pale light of the sunrise lit up the sky, making the immense cloud formations boiling out of the east seem that much darker by comparison. A storm followed them, traveling slowly, but inexorably. Some of the smaller clouds had broken away and had begun to pelt them with rain.

Aramis and Melchiades had continued out of the village and onto the path through the mountain on foot. They were being tailed by two people, though they did well to keep hidden. Mel had noticed the two follow them out of the inn. They didn't appear to be hostile. Their followers could have attacked them once they left the city, but so far they simply continued to follow them up the mountain.

"Who do you think they are?" Aramis asked. He was covered in sweat from the arduous climb. He kept wishing that a caravan would pass by and offer them a ride. He knew it wasn't likely. He paused for a moment to wipe the sweat from his face. He could tell that the uncovered areas of his skin were getting too much sun.

"I'm not sure. My first guess was Mordum's followers, but they'd have made their move already. We'll just have to keep going and see if they reveal themselves. Be ready, my Lord."

Aramis nodded in response. Unlike their trip to Mordum's shrine, at least now he had a sword. Mel had purchased it for him before they left. They continued their trek up the mountain, hoping to find someplace to take shelter before the main body of the storm hit. Mel informed him that flooding was a dangerous possibility where they were. They picked up the pace.

After an hour of climbing, they managed to reach the mountaintop right as the storm's fury crashed down upon them. The wind ripped furiously at their clothes and the driving rain pelted their skin. Aramis thought the raindrops felt like needles stabbing at him. Within minutes, tiny streams of water began running past them, carving paths through the dirt. Lightning flashed among the clouds and ground shaking thunder followed soon after. He faintly heard Mel say something over the thunder.

He shielded his eyes and looked at Mel, who stood hunched over bracing himself against the wind. He pointed and said something Aramis couldn't make out. He shrugged and followed his friend. The dirt under his feet had quickly become thick mud. It sucked at his boots, threatening to pull them off. His legs burned from the exertion.

The ground suddenly gave way and he fell forward, landing hard on his right shoulder. He cried out more in surprise than pain and struggled to get back up. The wind, rain, and mud made it almost impossible. He was so tired and his energy was flagging. Strong hands grabbed him and pulled him up. It was Mel. "I found a cave!" he shouted loudly, trying to be heard over the storm.

"Lead the way!" Aramis shouted back. They didn't walk far before Aramis saw the dark outline of the cave's entrance to their left. They angled themselves toward it, fighting against the wind that seemed likely to throw them down the mountain. They finally managed to stagger into the cave. Aramis slumped to the jagged rocky ground, exhausted.

Mel summoned his sword and walked further into the cave, disappearing into the darkness. A few moments later, he returned. Aramis looked up and Mel had his finger pressed against his lips.

"There's a bear in there," Mel said softly, motioning with his hand. "And she has cubs. If we stay quiet, we shouldn't bother them too much. The storm should pass by quickly judging by the power of the wind."

Aramis nodded wordlessly and unsheathed his sword. He set it beside him just in case. They sat resting in silence for several minutes before Aramis heard something. Instinctively, he grabbed his sword and stood up. Mel did the same. They positioned themselves on either side of the cave and away from the entrance. They didn't have to wait long before two figures staggered in.

"I swear they came this way," one of them said loudly.

Aramis looked to Mel and they both nodded. Simultaneously, they jumped from the shadows and each pointed a sword at one of the men. The one who had spoken yelped in surprise, brandishing his own blade astonishingly quick.

"Hold," the other figure spoke. From the tone, Aramis knew it was a man. His companion lowered his sword. "Prince Aramis, is that you?"

Aramis recognized the voice, but he couldn't see well enough in the gloom to determine if he recognized the man's face. "Who's asking?"

A soft glow suddenly illuminated the cave. Aramis

saw the light was coming from Mel's sword. His friend was full of surprises. His eyes widened in shock when he realized who the strangers were. "Lord Bavol," he said. "What are you doing here?"

Lord Bavol was an older man, with short white hair and pale blue eyes. He stood nearly the same height as Aramis but was a bit overweight. His stomach hung out over his belt. His clothes were stained from travel and he was dripping from the rain.

"Prince Aramis! Thank Zevea I found you!" The two men bowed low. "We've been scouring the entire country it seems. The court is in turmoil. The nobles are at odds, and there is a man claiming to be the new king!"

"Calm yourself," Aramis demanded, holding a hand up. "Slow down and tell me what is happening."

Bavol nodded. "I apologize, my Prince. Everyone knows the king is dead. Many rumors circulate the court, mainly that you killed him to take the throne. The nobles are divided. Some believe this tale, and some do not. I belong to the latter group."

"I appreciate your loyalty," Aramis replied. "You are right, I did not kill my father. He was assassinated before me as I struggled to defend him." Aramis's jaw tightened just thinking about it. He struggled to hold back the tears.

"We have had our differences in the past, but I would never believe you would have killed him. A few of the nobles agree with me, but many more have their doubts. The new 'king' isn't helping the matter. He's spewing accusations against you. He uses the fact that you are in hiding as his proof of your guilt."

Aramis fumed angrily. "Who is this man who claims to be king? I am the heir to the throne, and I am in hiding because I was being tortured in the dungeon like some sort of criminal!" Aramis stabbed his sword into the cave's floor. No one spoke. Aramis cupped his face in his hands and groaned, then looked back to Bavol.

"The man claims to be your elder brother. I don't trust him, though. He doesn't look respectable. He has some shady consorts as well. They all have a tattoo on their arms."

"A black cross?" It was Mel who spoke.

Bavol nodded. "Eric here was the first to notice and pointed it out to me. They are strange men and everyone seems to be afraid of them. My Prince, you must return to the castle and remove this charlatan."

"He can't," Mel said. "The guards are searching for us. What do you think would happen if he revealed himself? If they didn't kill him, they would lock him up. He cannot return without proof that he did not kill his father. That's why we are in hiding."

"He's right," Aramis chimed in. "I can't return. Not yet. We came across my father's assassin yesterday. We are trailing him. When I return, I will have proof."

"I'm afraid proof may not be enough, my Lord," Eric said. "The man has taken command of the army. This man will not forfeit the throne simply because you have proof that you didn't kill your father. You will need allies."

Bavol bit his lower lip. "Eric has a point; one I hadn't considered until now. If he controls the army and he doesn't intend to give up the throne, you'll have to take it by force. You will need your own army to do that."

"I will not make this kingdom a war-torn land like that of Talvaard," Aramis stated. "I grew up with the soldiers who served my father. I know where their loyalty lies, and it is not with some fool."

Mel cleared his throat. "My Prince. If this man consorts with the likes of Mordum's followers, the soldiers may not recognize you. Some of Mordum's priests are known to be able to control the minds of others. It would be wise to consider that this may end in violence."

Aramis considered Mel's words. He didn't want everything his father worked so hard to sustain to come crashing down in blood. Yet he couldn't control that outcome if he planned on taking his rightful place as king. "We will cross that bridge when—"

A loud roar echoed throughout the cave suddenly. They all turned to see a massive bear charging towards them. Aramis yanked his sword out of the ground and was about to charge the beast when Mel pushed him out of the way. He watched as Mel ran forward and slammed his magical blade into the ground. The air rippled around the sword and began to glow faintly. The bear slammed into the barrier and roared in frustration.

Mel turned around and shrugged. "I didn't want you to kill her," he said simply.

"Where can we get more of him?" Bavol asked in awe.

Aramis chuckled. "He follows Edria. His goddess is an enemy to Mordum. It's difficult to explain, but we will eventually have his order to aid in our fight against Mordum."

They watched the bear stalk back and forth in front of the barrier, occasionally growling at them. It was silent for a few moments and then Aramis spoke. "Lord Bavol, I need you to go back to the court and sway as many of the nobles as possible to our cause. I will find allies where I can, and when I return we will remove this man from the throne."

"I will do everything I can, my Prince. Allow my servant Eric to go with you. He will help you with anything you need."

"I thank you for the offer, but I fear he will only slow us down. He is not a soldier and where we travel will be dangerous. Keep your servant with you. Eric will serve our cause better in the court than on the road with me."

Aramis looked out of the cave's entrance. "The storm is letting up. Lord Bavol, you should go now. Mel and I need to get back on the road as well. We have many things to do, and time is quickly passing."

"May Zevea watch over you," Bavol said. He bowed low and turned to Eric. "Let us be on our way." They left the cave and headed back down the mountain toward Oakvalor.

"We have one problem," Mel said.

"What?"

"The bear. Once I remove my sword, the barrier will fade. We'll have to run like never before."

Aramis nodded in agreement. "So be it," he said.

Mel grabbed his sword, turned, and they ran as fast as they could.

CHAPTER 15

Aramis found Talvaard to be not so unlike his own kingdom. Having grown up his entire life knowing they were at war with their neighboring kingdom, he had always assumed the place was … different. But what he found was that the people were just like his own. They tended their fields, worked various jobs, and went about their daily lives.

Aside from the many battle-destroyed sites that littered the land, he couldn't tell the difference between the two kingdoms. He had heard rumors that the kingdom was engulfed in civil war, but what he and Mel encountered was much worse than something written in a report.

The first few towns they came across were nothing more than burned out husks. They had seen only a few people in those places, and none of them would answer their questions, let alone look at them. The horrors of war were being revealed to Aramis in a very real way. Aramis had decided that although they were on a time-sensitive mission, they would help the people of Talvaard where they could.

In one of the towns, they had spent an entire day digging graves and helping bury the dead. Once they were finished, they were treated by some of the townspeople with a bath and warm food. Aramis was surprised that Mel didn't complain about getting so dirty and said as much.

"Simply because I enjoy the aristocratic way of life, doesn't mean I don't also enjoy doing good. I am a priest of Edria for a reason, my Lord."

"I didn't mean to offend you, Mel. I was only jesting with you."

"You did not offend me. I can understand why you would think that, however. I do enjoy the court probably more than I should."

The next morning as they were getting ready to head out, they were greeted by one of the townspeople.

"Morning, gents. I've got a message for you from the general who oversees this town. He'd like to meet with both of you."

Aramis was wary. They had already lost a good deal of time, and he didn't want to get drawn into the political battle being waged in Talvaard. "I'm afraid we must get back on the road. Can you tell the general that we were in a hurry and perhaps on our way back through we can meet with him?"

"I could do that. But you may want to make time to meet with him now. He wants to thank you for helping us. General Garrick is a man of honor. He has always defended our city from vagabonds and orc raiders. His army is now stretched thin trying to defend so many from the other generals who simply want to take the throne. He tried to stay out of the battles, but the others continued to attack his province. It took the blessing of the townsfolk to get him to join the fray."

Aramis listened intently. This General Garrick sounded like a man whom he could trust. He looked to Mel for advice, but Mel only offered a shrug as if to say 'it's your decision'.

"We will go now," Aramis decided.

The man smiled. "Great! Follow me. He arrived in town just this morning after receiving news that our town was sacked." The man led them to one of the few buildings left mostly unscathed. Aramis couldn't tell what kind of building it was. Two thin posts hung above the entrance, but the sign that should have been hanging from them was missing. Aramis assumed it had been knocked off during the town's attack, but it was impossible to be sure.

The man led them into the building which turned out to be a tavern. It was dark inside except for a few candles and lanterns. The windows were covered with dark sheets that managed to blot out almost all of the sunlight.

"Wait here," the man said. He made his way to a table where several armored men sat. They hadn't waited long before the man returned and directed them to the table. As they approached, one of the men stood up to greet them.

His plate armor was a deep onyx color. It was also covered in dents and scrapes. Aramis thought he could see spots of blood as well. The man's face was a dark tan color, and his hair was almost as dark as his armor. He smiled as they approached the table.

"Thank you for meeting with me. I hope this will not delay you too much?"

Everything about the man exuded a sense of dignity and humility. His bearing was that of a strong leader, but his voice was soft. The man almost reminded him of his father.

"It's no trouble," Aramis replied. "We do have

pressing business, but it can wait."

The man nodded. "These men are my Captains. I don't mean to be rude, but they are about to leave with their orders. You are all dismissed." All five Captains stood up and left the tavern. "Please sit," Garrick bade them. They both did as he asked. "Would you like anything to eat or drink?"

"No, thank you," Aramis answered. "Your people have taken care of us already."

Garrick smiled again. "Good. I've asked you two to meet with me because the people of the town told me how you helped them. I am indebted to you. When I heard that the town was attacked, I rode all night to get here."

A young girl approached the table and set a wooden cup down in front of Garrick. He took a sip and looked to the girl. "This is perfect, thank you." The girl curtsied and disappeared into the kitchen.

"As a man who strives to protect my people, I have many agents in many places. As such, I know a great deal more about people than they know about me." Garrick took another drink from his cup. "So tell me, how do the Prince of Oakvalor and his servant come to be in Talvaard?"

Aramis's mouth gaped in surprise. He wasn't sure how to answer. The man seemed trustable, but how much should he reveal? He was thankful when Mel spoke up.

"We are on a quest to retrieve something that was stolen from us."

"I see," he said, frowning. "And these thieves are in my province?"

"Most of them were killed in a rockslide in the Viss Mountains. The one who stole from us escaped. We are not sure where he is exactly. We only know he came through the mountains and crossed into Talvaard.

Perhaps you may have seen him? He wears robes and has a black cross tattoo on his left arm."

"I'm sorry, but I have not seen anyone like that. You must be Melchiades, correct?"

Mel tilted his head in a bow. "I am."

Garrick looked to Aramis. "Do you trust Melchiades?"

"With my life," Aramis answered.

"Very well. We can speak freely then. I know the rumor in Oakvalor has spread quickly that you have killed your father. There is always a seed of truth in a rumor, but I would rather hear it from the one who was there."

Aramis cleared his throat. "My father is dead, but I did not kill him. The man we are searching for didn't just steal from us, he is also my father's assassin."

"I am sorry to hear that," Garrick said. "Your father was a good man."

"You knew my father?" Aramis asked.

"I did not meet him directly, no. But I did correspond with him by letter when my own king was alive. They were working on a peace treaty by marriage … and I'm sure we all know how that went." Garrick shook his head sadly.

"Yes. My sister was killed and both of your princes died."

Garrick nodded. "The people of my country haven't even had proper time to grieve the loss. The other generals and some of the nobles began fighting over the throne immediately. It has become brother against brother, family against family."

"I fear that my own kingdom will look like this," Aramis said softly.

"What do you mean?" Garrick asked.

"I've been accused of murdering my father and a man has usurped the throne in my absence. I'm trying to track down the assassin to prove my innocence, yet this false king is adding to the rumors about me. The longer it takes me to find this man, the more damage is done. I fear my own kingdom will fall to pieces as yours has."

"You have a hard road before you; that is true. Tell me though, why did you help the people here? Our kingdoms have been at war for longer than anyone can remember. You are searching for an assassin and you probably could have tracked him down by now, so what made you stop and give time you didn't have to these people?"

"I saw in them my own people," Aramis answered. "I've grown up believing the people here were cruel and wanted only to fight. I've seen otherwise. These people just want to live their lives in peace as my own do. Helping them bury their dead was the least I could do to make amends for my forefathers' mistakes."

"You will make a good king," Garrick said. "I appreciate what you have done here for my people. In return, I will do something for you. Though I have not seen this man you spoke of, I do know a place where people with these tattoos congregate. I will give you a map to this place."

"You do more for us than we have done for your people," Aramis said. "This will put us one step closer to proving my innocence."

"I believe you are innocent. I would like to propose something to you. You don't have to decide now. The war here will be coming to an end soon. If you will give me your support, I will give you mine. Make a public endorsement in favor of me being king of Talvaard, and I will help you get your throne back."

"I'm sorry, but I don't understand how my endorsement of you would help. Technically we are enemies. If anything, I would think the people here would see that as a bad sign."

Garrick nodded. "Let me try to explain. I did not want anything to do with this war. But at the urging of my people, I fought back against the others who were doing nothing but terrorizing their own kingdom. The men you saw earlier, my Captains? They were generals fighting against me not long ago. I defeated their armies and took their cities. Now they follow me without question. I have reunified the majority of the kingdom. There is only one who continues to fight. He is a violent man, prone to drunkenness.

"If I can show the people that our long-time enemy Oakvalor has given me the blessing to rule and backs me with support, I will be able to unify the entire country back under one banner. No more civil war, no more pointless fighting. The only man left causing strife may even surrender without any more bloodshed. I desire peace and my people desire peace. That is all I want."

Aramis digested everything. It made sense. "So all you want me to do is say I approve of you being king? That seems much less effort than it does for you to help me get my throne back. I feel like I would owe you something I cannot repay."

Garrick waved his hand. "Nonsense. We both want what is best for our people. All I ask is that we help each other bring peace and stability back to our kingdoms. Once we have accomplished that, we can finally create the peace treaty that has been a long time coming. As I said, you don't have to answer now. Think about it and let me know when you come back through with the proof your people need. If I am not here, you can leave me a message here at this tavern and I will get it."

"May I speak with my friend in private?" Aramis asked.

"Of course," Garrick said.

Aramis and Mel rose from the table and retreated toward the entrance. Aramis was thinking through everything. It seemed the right course of action, especially since it would give him the military support he would need to take his throne back if it came down to it. "What do you think, Mel?"

"It is your decision, my Prince. I would not want to sway you one way or another."

"I think I should do it. The man seems honorable and level-headed. You said yourself that we should be prepared in the event that I have to take the throne by force. He has an army that he is willing to lend me. This is an opportunity to not only get support to take the throne back but also to end the conflict between our two kingdoms."

"I see it the same way. I just didn't want to sway your opinion if you were against the idea. Though he didn't say he would lend you his army. He only said he would help you. You may want to clarify that point."

They walked back to the table and took their seats. Garrick took a drink from his cup.

"I fear the man who usurped my throne will not leave without a fight. Does your support include your army, if it is needed?" Aramis asked.

"I will give you anything I can to aid you. Supplies, men, weapons. Whatever you need."

"Then we have an agreement," Aramis said. He reached across the table and grabbed Garrick's hand.

"Agreed," Garrick said with a smile. And they shook hands. "I will need my messengers to carry the letter of your support to every city. Can you provide a letter now?"

"If you have parchment and ink, I can pen it before we leave."

Garrick summoned the young girl from the kitchen and told her what he needed. She left and returned shortly after, bringing several pieces of parchment, a quill, and an inkwell. Aramis wrote out a letter of support and signed it. He slid the paper to Garrick, who read it and nodded in satisfaction.

"Excellent. I asked the girl to have one of my Captains bring the map I told you about. He should be here in a moment."

They didn't wait long before the man arrived and delivered the map. He handed it to Garrick and left. Garrick unfolded it and looked it over, then gave it to Aramis.

"The black square is our current position. The line that leads west is the road you will need to take. It is a long journey even by horseback, so make sure you have all of the supplies you need. The people will provide you with whatever you need. I believe there is a carriage if you need one. With that said, may you find success. I look forward to seeing you again, King Aramis."

● ∞ ● ∞ ●

Aramis and Mel had been fortunate enough to find the carriage. Judging by the map, it would take them several weeks to reach their destination. The place Garrick described was on the edge of Talvaard, close to the unmapped regions beyond. They loaded the carriage with enough food and water for two weeks. Aramis wanted to take more, but there was only so much space.

"We can find game to hunt if we run low on food," Mel said. "According to the map, there aren't any cities that far west. Just forests and flatlands."

A week into their journey brought bad news. They were both sleeping when the carriage jostled about harshly, waking them up. Aramis could hear the driver cursing. "We'd better see what happened," he said. They stepped out of the carriage into a rainstorm. Within moments they were drenched.

"What happened?" Mel asked the driver, using his

hands to keep the rain out of his eyes.

"The blasted wheel hit a rut and cracked in two," the driver answered.

"Is there a replacement?" Mel asked.

The driver shook his head. "No. If I can't repair the wheel, I'll have to head back and get one. It could take a couple of weeks if they have to build a new one." Aramis looked to Mel helplessly.

"When will you know if you can fix it?" Mel asked.

"As soon as the rain lets up. I can't apply anything while the wood is wet. You two should get back in the carriage and wait. I'll let you know."

Not knowing how they could help, they did as the driver said and climbed back into the carriage. "This isn't good," Aramis said. "If he can't fix the wheel, we will lose even more time. It's taking too long to get there as it is."

"I know, my Lord. We should have a plan in the event that repairing the wheel isn't going to work. We could take the horses and continue on. They can carry more than we can on foot. Aside from that, I don't see many options that don't put us farther behind. We're also assuming the templar is going to this place Garrick mentioned, but we don't know that for sure."

Aramis covered his face in his hands and rested his back against the soft cushions. "This isn't happening," he muttered. "Mel, tell me this isn't happening. Tell me this is all a horrible dream."

"I wish that I could, my Lord."

Aramis didn't know how much time had passed, but the door to the carriage opened and the driver peeked his head in. "I'm sorry, but I'm unable to repair the wheel. I'm going to head back to town and see about getting a replacement. You're welcome to come along, or you can wait here if it suits you."

"I think we will stay here," Mel said. "But you may

want to bring some horses back as well."

"Why?" the driver asked.

"Because we are taking these ones. Don't worry about coming to get us. We'll be back when we are finished with our business."

"Very well. Safe travels to you." The driver shut the door.

"Looks like we better get packing," Mel said. Aramis nodded wordlessly. They exited the carriage and saw the driver had already started walking back toward the town. Mel unhitched the horses and Aramis began loading their supplies. They packed more food than water, as the map showed a few streams and rivers located along their route.

They mounted the horses and continued west, following the map and taking note of points of interest and traveled until dusk, then made camp next to a stand of trees. They ate a small meal and took turns keeping watch as the other slept. In the morning, they continued on. The same routine followed until the days had blurred into weeks.

After almost a month, they finally came across signs of people. A few scattered campsites at first, then makeshift shelters. They traveled warily, looking everywhere to make sure there were no guards or scouts. Their food supply had exhausted weeks ago and they relied on berries and small animals to hold them over. Being on the road so long had made them irritable. The signs that they were almost there gave them some excitement.

"According to the map, there is a clearing on the other side of these trees. In the clearing is where the followers of Mordum are supposed to gather," Mel said.

"We're almost done with this madness," Aramis growled.

They dismounted and tied their horses to one of the

trees. Aramis grabbed his sword from the saddle and sheathed it as his side. They walked quietly through the woods, trying to avoid stepping on anything that might make a sound.

Suddenly the world went upside down. Aramis cried out in surprise as he and Mel were hanging above the ground in a net. They struggled but were unable to free themselves. Giving up, Aramis looked down to see how they had managed to walk into this trap.

And standing there looking up at them was his father's killer.

"To forget the dead would be akin to killing them a second time."

—Prince Aramis

CHAPTER 16

Fourteen Years Ago

Jovanna stared at the flowers that seemed to represent every color one could imagine. Vibrant reds, oranges, blues, and purples that came in all sizes and oddly beautiful shapes. The flower shop was one of her favorite places to visit in the market.

She never bought any of them, though her father would bring them to her mother sometimes, usually after they had argued about something. As she walked around the shop, she noticed a flower she hadn't seen before. It was tall and bright yellow.

"What is this one?" she asked the lady who owned the shop.

The owner came around the desk she was standing behind to take a look. "Ah," she said with a smile. "That's a day lily."

"I've never seen one before. Did you just get it?"

"Yes, it arrived today. They don't naturally grow in this part of the country. I'm going to see if I can change that. How's your mother doing?"

Jovanna shrugged, still staring at the flower. "She's well. She and father had another fight last night. I'm guessing he'll come by here to get her some of these. It's how he says he's sorry." The owner nodded and went back to her work behind the desk. "I'm going to head home now. Mother will get worried if I'm not home before my father."

"Give your mother my regards," the owner said.

"I will," Jovanna answered as she left. She walked along the cobblestone paved streets, enjoying the sights and smells of everything as was her custom. Being the only child of a poorer family, she wasn't expected to do much. Jovanna had tried school, but she didn't like it. She wasn't like the other children and didn't feel like she fit in. Since schooling was free, her mother didn't complain too much.

"I want you to be smart as well as happy," her mother had said when she found out Jovanna wasn't going back to the school. "Going to school may not make you happy, but it will make you smart. They'll teach you things you won't learn otherwise."

"You didn't go to school. And neither did father. Why should I?"

"So that you can be successful in whatever you decide to do. So that if you leave this town, you can go anywhere you want."

Jovanna laughed. "Why would I want to leave? You and father have never left. And I wouldn't want to leave you anyway."

Her mother had simply shaken her head and said, "You'll understand when you are older."

She didn't understand adults. They didn't like to have fun and they were always so serious. Didn't they know they were kids once too? As she passed the bakery, the scent of freshly baked bread greeted her. She breathed in deep, savoring it. Jovanna continued along the road until it became a dirt path. Her house was on the outskirts of the town.

As she entered the house, her mother was coming out of her sewing room. "I was starting to wonder where you were," her mother said. "You are usually here earlier."

"I was at the flower shop," she answered. "The owner got a new flower in and it's beautiful!" Her mother smiled at her enthusiasm.

"Carina is too busy for you to be bothering her every day."

"I don't bother her. I just look at her flowers."

"Did you see your father while you were there?"

Jovanna shook her head. "I told her he'd probably come by to get you flowers because you had a fight."

"Why did you tell her that? Please don't repeat those things. And how did you know we argued? You were asleep."

"I told her because it's true. And I was asleep until I heard father yelling."

"Just because it's true doesn't mean you have to say it," her mother admonished.

"Really?" Jovanna beamed.

"You know what I mean," her mother said, pointing her finger playfully. "Now go get ready for dinner. Your father will be home any minute."

Jovanna ran to do as she was told. Since she hadn't played in the dirt with any of the other kids in town, she really didn't need to wash her hands. She took her shoes off and changed into her sleeping clothes. When dinner was finished she would go to bed, so she liked to be prepared.

After she had changed, she met her mother in the kitchen and sat down at the table. Her mother placed a bowl in front of her that was steaming. She looked in the bowl: mashed potatoes, gravy, and small pieces of meat all mixed together. She blew on the food several times before she went to take a bite.

"Don't eat yet," he mother said. "You need to wait for your father."

"Yes mother," Jovanna groaned. She was hungry and didn't want to wait. She snuck a few bites while her mother wasn't looking. A few minutes later, her father arrived. He came in and went to clean himself up, then came into the kitchen. He threw himself into the chair he always sat in.

"What's wrong?" her mother asked.

"The crops are bad this year," father responded. He rubbed his face with his hands and closed his eyes. "It's going to be a rough year."

"Last year was rough but we survived," mother replied. She placed a bowl before him and then sat down at the table with her own bowl.

"I'm tired of just *surviving*," father said. "For once I would like things to go well for us and to enjoy life." He took a bite of his food and chewed in silence.

"Things will get better," mother said, smiling at him. "Things can only get better."

Her father slammed his fist onto the table. "Stop being so positive!" he yelled. "Things are horrible. They've been horrible and they are only going to stay that way! If you think your comments are helping, they aren't. Just shut your mouth."

Jovanna could tell her mother was trying to hold back her tears. The rest of the meal was oppressively quiet. As she went to her room to go to bed, she realized her father didn't bring any flowers back. "But he always brings flowers," she whispered to herself. She fell asleep troubled.

● ∞ ● ∞ ●

The next morning, she woke to find her mother

sewing and her father had gone to work the fields. Everything seemed like normal. She shrugged and left the house, walking to the market area to see what new things the merchants had.

She made her normal rounds, checking out the jewelry and clothing vendors. She loved spending time in the market and the time always seemed to pass by so quickly. Before she knew it, it was almost time to head home. She stopped at the flower shop and took in the sights and smells. Carina was watering some flowers that looked like they weren't doing so well. She greeted Jovanna and continued working.

"Did my father come by yesterday?" she asked.

"He didn't," Carina answered without looking up. She was pulling dead leaves off some of the flowers. "Perhaps he forgot."

"Father never forgets to bring flowers," she answered. She stood before the day lily, admiring its beauty. "He should bring her this one. It will make mother's day. It's so beautiful," she said wistfully. Carina looked at her thoughtfully. She came over to stand beside her.

"It is beautiful," Carina agreed. She put the flower into a smaller vase and handed it to Jovanna. "Take it to your mother."

Jovanna shook her head. "I don't have any money," she said.

"Don't worry about that," Carina answered. "Just take it to her. If you think she will love it, then she should have it. This will be our little surprise."

Jovanna's smile encompassed her entire face. "Really? Thank you! You are the nicest person I know!"

Carina smiled. "No, thank *you*."

Jovanna left, holding the vase tightly so that she wouldn't drop it. When she finally reached her house, she hid the flower from her mother and waited for her father to get home. When he did, she noticed that he hadn't brought anything back for her mother again.

She decided to surprise her mother with the flower by making her think that her father had brought it. While her father cleaned up for dinner, she brought the flower into the kitchen and placed it on the table while her mother wasn't looking.

Father entered the kitchen and sat down tiredly in his chair. He looked at the flower on the table but didn't say anything. Her mother brought their plates to the table and paused when she saw the flower. She smiled and finished setting the plates down.

"How was the work today?" mother asked.

Father grunted in reply. That usually meant he was too tired to talk about it. They ate in silence again like the night before, only this time it wasn't awkward. She saw her mother smiling at the flower while she ate. Her father was looking at it also. For some reason, Jovanna didn't like the way he was looking at it. After she had finished eating, she went to her room. She fell asleep happy to know that she made her mother smile by bringing the flower home.

Yelling woke her up. She sat up in her bed, wondering why her parents would be fighting again. She slipped out of bed and quietly stood outside their bedroom. They were standing on opposite sides of the bed. Her mother's face was streaked with tears and her father looked angry.

"Tell me who it was," father demanded.

"I told you already," mother sobbed. "There isn't anyone."

"Then where did the flower come from?" he asked.

"I don't know," mother answered. "I thought you had brought it for me."

"You are lying," father said. "Tell me who he is."

Jovanna wasn't sure what they were talking about.

Were they fighting over the flower? Jovanna bit her lip in worry. She didn't want to get in trouble for it. She only tried to make things better.

"I'm not lying," mother said. "I really thought you brought it for me."

Father glared at her and clenched his fist. Jovanna had never seen him so enraged before. "Stop lying to me," he said through gritted teeth. "I didn't bring it for you."

Her mother began weeping uncontrollably. "I'm not lying to you," she said brokenly. "I swear to you there isn't another man. I love you."

Her father stormed quickly across the room and grabbed her mother, slamming her violently into the wall several times. "Don't you dare say that to me after what you've done!" he screamed madly. Jovanna backed away from the door, frightened by what she saw. Father slammed her into the wall one more time before letting go of her. Her body slumped lifelessly down the wall and onto the floor, leaving a trail of smeared blood.

"Get up," father said. The anger in his voice seemed to have lessened, replaced by something else. Was it … worry? "Get up," he said again, gently this time. He kneeled down beside her and touched her face. "Please wake up," he said. He shook her a bit before becoming frantic.

Jovanna turned and fled back to her room. She hid under the blankets and cried bitterly. She cried until she eventually fell back to sleep.

When she woke up, it was morning. She slowly got out of bed and looked around the room. She had the scariest dream. Leaving the room, she went into the kitchen. Her mother hadn't made breakfast yet. That was odd. A feeling of dread came over her as she walked toward the sewing room. She hesitated, then pushed the door open. It was empty.

She went to her parents' bedroom and opened the door. Lying on the floor was her mother's body. She gasped.

It wasn't a dream at all!

She cried as she ran to her mother's body. Her skin had become pale. A puddle of blood surrounded her, most likely from the wound on the back of her head.

She ran from the room, looking for her father. "Father!" she screamed. "Father!" The house appeared to be empty. She opened the front door and found her father. His lifeless body hung from a rope attached to the awning of their porch. She screamed in horror.

● ∞ ● ∞ ●

When her father didn't show up at the fields for work, some of the other workers came to the house to see where he was. Upon finding his body, the entire house became a place of chaos. The workers had found Jovanna in her room wrapped in a ball crying hysterically.

The city guard was called in to investigate and clean up the bodies. They tried to get Jovanna to talk about what happened, but the only thing she said was, "I killed them."

"She's traumatized," one of the guards told another. "It's highly doubtful she actually killed them. It looks like the man killed his wife, then hung himself. The poor girl."

A few hours later, someone from an orphanage came and took her away from the only home she had ever known.

CHAPTER 17

Jovanna watched the elves from the vantage of a small hill. The sun was setting but still burned brightly, causing her to sweat more than she cared to. Velent and his warriors were in similar positions along the hilltop. The enemy appeared to be finishing setting up their camp and preparing to settle in for the night. Jovanna had seen many war camps in her time, and this one was no different.

Tents made of animal hides were sprawled out in all directions. At one of them, several elves were being tattooed by some elders. Another tent served as the meal area and had a small line of elves gathered. This force was much larger than the one they encountered in the village four days previously. Even though they were massively outnumbered, Jovanna counted the number of Velent's warriors.

Eighteen.

She turned her gaze back to the war camp. Eighteen against close to what looked like a thousand. They wouldn't even likely put a dent in those numbers. All she needed was to find their leader, the one who was responsible for Jerik's death. She would kill him and then … and then what?

The thought made her freeze for a moment. What would she do after she avenged the old man who had saved her life? She forced the thought from her mind. That wasn't important right now. She could hear Velent instructing his warriors.

"Once the night is upon us, we will sneak into their camp. Tent by tent, we will kill as many as possible. We must not be seen or caught. In one hour, we will meet back here. If you aren't here, I will assume you are dead or dying. Am I clear? Good. Take your positions."

He didn't bother giving her any direction. She didn't need it either way. She continued scanning the tents in the waning light, looking for anything that resembled a command post. Eventually, the sun was gone and she still hadn't found it. "I'll search them all if I have to," she muttered to the darkness. She waited and watched as the guards switched out. It was time.

She made her way down the hill as stealthy as possible, pausing here and there to make sure she wasn't seen. It was dark, but the elves had a perimeter of torches and the moon was shining brightly. She got past the first two guards easily. They were playing a traditional elven game called *dueling*. The game was played with several small sticks that had various symbols inscribed on the ends. Each player would then throw the sticks down and hope that two matching symbols landed on each other.

Jovanna thought it was a waste of time as the winner didn't get anything. At least the humans knew how to properly gamble. They were so focused on the game they didn't notice her slink by in the shadows. She entered a large tent and found two elves sleeping. She quickly slit their throats and slipped out, looking for another large tent. She saw several, but none of them housed the leader. After killing thirty elves, she was starting to get frustrated. The war camp was large and only semi-organized.

She was about to make a rash decision and cause a commotion to see if she could draw him out when a horn split the air suddenly. It was followed by another, and then a third one. The camp burst to life and warriors began running toward the western side of the camp. She cursed, knowing that Velent or one of his warriors had probably been caught.

Jovanna waited until she didn't see any other elves before leaving the tent she was in. She jogged through the camp, trailing a few of the warriors. She rounded a tent and almost bumped into a group of them. She quickly entered another one of the tents to keep from being seen.

Cutting a slit in the back of the tent, she looked out to see what was happening. It looked like the entire camp had gathered. She couldn't see enough to know if one of Velent's men had been caught or not. She heard someone talking loudly, but she wasn't able to hear what was being said.

"What's going on?" one of the elves asked.

"War council," another answered.

"How do you know?" the first one asked.

"I can hear him speaking," the other answered.

"You got Wolf Ears?"

The other elf nodded.

Jovanna's face scrunched in confusion. *Wolf Ears?* She hadn't heard of that tattoo before. She made a mental note to research it.

"He says we leave at first light to invade the human cities," Wolf Ears said.

The other smiled. "Good. It is time we take our lands

back."

She listened to their conversation a little longer and then decided she needed to get moving. As she moved to leave the tent, she realized that one of the beds was occupied. She went in for the kill before she noticed the elf was already dead. She grunted softly, knowing Velent's men would be somewhere close by. The tent opened and an elf stepped in.

Giving little thought to it, she pushed the dead elf to the edge of the bed and laid down in his place. Immediately she felt the warm blood soaking through her shirt. She shuddered as a memory came back to her, the darkest part of her childhood. The elf who entered the tent brought her back to the present.

"You didn't go to the council," he said. It sounded more like an accusation than a question. She didn't respond.

"Tairu won't stand for rebelliousness. You know better than I what he will do to those who stand in his way. Make sure you are ready in the morning. We march for Talvaard." He climbed into his own bed. Jovanna waited until she heard him breathing evenly, then she got up. So the elves *were* marching into the human kingdoms. And who was this Tairu?

She had not heard the name before. She considered the possibility that Tairu was their leader. He appeared to instill fear in these warriors. Jovanna hadn't spent long with the elves, but she did know that fear was not something they generally showed. She decided that Tairu must be the leader who had united the tribes. She left the tent and wandered the camp a little longer, still looking for the command post. Since the horns had woken everyone up, however, it was much harder moving about the camp. She finally decided to leave and meet back with Velent and his men.

Jovanna made her way out of the camp and back up

the hill to where they had been before. Velent met her as she crested the hill. "You were down there longer than an hour."

"I wasn't aware I had instructions," Jovanna replied. "You didn't seem eager to share your plan with me, so I did what I felt was prudent."

"I knew you were listening," he said, his tone revealing his growing impatience.

"Did you learn anything?" she asked.

"What?"

"I don't like repeating myself," she answered.

Velent scowled at her. "No. We didn't."

"I figured as much. When I heard the horns, I thought for sure you or one of your warriors had slipped up and gotten caught."

He spat at her feet. "*Please*. You aren't half of what my weakest warrior is. *I* thought *you* had messed up down there."

"Do you want to test that statement?" she asked, resting her hand on the hilt of her sword.

He ignored her threat. "Did *you* learn anything?" he asked mockingly.

"You know I did," she said.

"Lies."

"Have you heard of an elf named Tairu?" she asked casually, looking up into the sky.

"That isn't funny," he replied.

Jovanna noticed a change in his demeanor. "What do you mean?"

Velent continued to glare at her.

Jovanna was curious now. "I honestly don't know what you are talking about. I've never heard the name until tonight." She thought for a moment he didn't believe her and would walk away. After a bit of silence, he responded.

"Tairu was a powerful warrior of my tribe," he began

hesitantly. "His tattoos were strong … his skill with weapons was unparalleled. He quickly gained favor in the tribe and was elevated to War Chief. Our tribe became highly respected and another Tribe Chief offered his daughter to Tairu for his wife. The woman refused him, so Tairu killed her. As is the custom, when one tribe affronts another, the offended tribe can declare war. Instead of doing that, the Tribe Chief told my father to banish Tairu and there would be peace."

"That doesn't seem like a fair trade. A daughter for a warrior? I know women aren't as valued as men in the tribes, but it was his daughter." Jovanna knew there was more to the story. "The chief demanded that to strip your father of his prized warrior, didn't he?"

"That may have been part of his reasoning," Velent replied, "but it was fair. Tairu was my brother, the eldest of us. One family member for another."

"Why didn't I know this already?"

"Other than the fact that you are a *human* and it is none of your concern?" Jovanna could tell he was forcing the sarcasm. "When someone is banished, they are forgotten. Their name can never be spoken again. This is why."

Before she could say anything, he turned to walk away. "Velent," she called after him. "The army down there is marching for Talvaard at first light." He just kept walking. She shrugged and looked out at the war camp. She needed a way to get near Tairu.

● ∞ ● ∞ ●

After a few hours, Jovanna headed back into the camp. The excitement of the warriors had finally subsided. She found a tent with only a single warrior and killed him. She was careful not to get the blood on his clothes. She managed to remove his shirt and replace her own dirty one. She hid the body in another tent and waited for morning.

As the sun crested the horizon, horns rang out across the camp. It was time to get moving. Jovanna rubbed the sleep from her eyes. She had intended to stay up through the rest of the night in case something happened. Apparently, nothing had. She drew her sword and looked at her reflection. Her illusion was still holding up.

She left the tent and fell into step with the other warriors as they began forming into ranks. Her stomach growled and she wondered if the elves would eat breakfast before they began their march. They waited for almost an hour as all the warriors got into their positions. As soon as the stragglers had joined the multitude, other elves began breaking down the camp.

At first, she thought the elves were captives, but then she saw that they were women. *I thought Velent said women don't go to war,* she thought. Whoever this Tairu was, he was obviously going against tradition. Other groups of women ran through the ranks of warriors handing out food. Jovanna was given two dry biscuits and a cooked lizard. As soon as she choked it down, the elves began marching.

Jovanna analyzed their skills and methods as they traveled toward Talvaard's border. They certainly weren't trained like men were. Everything she had seen in the armies of men was seriously lacking here. But the elves had something the humans didn't. Tattoo magic. Their spells were some of the most powerful magic she had ever beheld.

Outside the walls of Palindrom, as the dragon possessed prince was leading his armies, she had witnessed a single elf obliterate the soul of the dragon. If the humans thought they were up against tribal barbarians, they had a rude awakening coming.

They marched most of the day and didn't take many

breaks. Jovanna guessed they had traveled a substantial distance when they paused at the outskirts of a large city. Protective walls surrounded the place and she wondered how the elves would break through the defenses. In the distance, she could see the guards on the walls looking their way. She wondered briefly what they might be thinking.

An order was shouted from one of the formation leaders and several elves sprinted toward the city. Jovanna watched curiously. As the elves neared the walls, some of their tattoos began to glow. They threw themselves into the walls and they exploded. Her eyes widened in surprise. Why would they sacrifice their warriors to break through the walls? As the smoke and debris cleared, she saw the elves had blown holes in the walls.

Commotion rang out in the city and Jovanna realized the elves hadn't sacrificed themselves after all. They had merely used their tattoos to blast through the walls.

"Clever," she said to herself. It wouldn't work every time, especially once the humans learned of the trick. They would cut the elves down from the walls with crossbows or ballistae. But for now, it worked. The captains shouted and the ranks of elves surged toward the city. Jovanna tried to hang back so she could find where Tairu was.

It was impossible to weave through the mass of bodies and she was forced forward with the army. Other elves worked to make the holes in the walls larger so the warriors could get into the city faster. Jovanna tried desperately to remove herself from the flow, but she was forced into the walls as well. The city's guards had gathered at the blasted portions of the walls and were fighting with the elves trying to enter.

Jovanna drew her sword as she was forced toward the guards. It was utter chaos. The clash of steel and the screams of the dying filled the air. Blood had already begun to cover the streets and Jovanna almost slipped. She stepped over the bodies of the fallen and tried to evade the guards. They were overcome with adrenaline and were hacking and slashing wildly, careless of the safety of their fellows.

Jovanna managed to get to the outer edge of the elvish line, but a group of guards came running from the inner part of the city to join the fray. They were coming right at her. Jovanna considered every option. Unfortunately, there weren't many. If she released her illusions, the elves would try to cut her down because she was human. If she kept the illusion, the guards would try to kill her because she was an elf.

Something inside her broke and she rushed forward, attacking the guards. She demolished their ranks and cut through them with ease. She hacked arms off and crushed kneecaps with her foot. She sliced through helmets and armor, killing with an animal like ferocity.

When her blood lust finally abated, she stood in the midst of a pile of bodies, both elves and men. Her body heaved as she breathed hard and surveyed the damage. She had taken a few cuts along her arms and legs, but nothing serious. The elves had overrun the city and the humans were on the run.

Jovanna knelt beside one of the guards and pulled his helm off. She felt a horrible wrench in her gut as she saw the guard couldn't have been older than fifteen. His face was covered with blood, but she could still see the look of terror on his face. And she had killed him. She turned her head and vomited, sickened by what she had done.

"What's wrong with me?" she growled. She had never shied away from battle or death. Why was this any different? *He's just a kid*, she thought, answering her own question. She stood up and staggered through the carnage to lean up against one of the buildings nearby.

She took several deep breaths and tried to calm herself. She didn't like this feeling. She *hated* this feeling.

She looked up as a group of elves entered the blasted walls. She recognized some of them as the formation leaders. One of them walked with a different bearing. He projected strength and authority. It looked like the elf she had battled with when Jerik was killed. She knew without a doubt this was Tairu.

She wiped the sweat from her face. They weren't even looking her way. *This is it*, she thought, *this is where he dies*. She gripped the hilt of her sword tightly and walked calmly toward him.

"Character is not made in crisis, it is only exhibited."

—Melchiades

CHAPTER 18

Aramis strained against his bonds, but it was no use. The ropes were cutting into his wrists and he could feel that his hands were sticky from the blood. Directly across from him, Mel was in a similar situation. They were each tied to a tall wooden pole. He looked over to his friend and thought he was sleeping, but then he noticed Mel's lips were moving.

"Why is he praying at a time like this?" Aramis whispered to himself. He looked around the courtyard they were in. There were several of the wooden poles sticking up out of the ground, but he and Mel were the only prisoners. A few of the poles were stained red from what Aramis assumed was blood. The courtyard was on the outer edge of the temple complex.

Aramis had been surprised to find that the location of Mordum's followers wasn't a camp as he had suspected, but a small city. At the northern end stood the massive building made of dark gray stone that served as a temple. It was foreboding and Aramis found it to be nightmarish. Ghoulish creatures decorated the outside. The entire place radiated evil. The temple was backed against a series of hills too small to be considered mountains. The front area was a decently sized courtyard, surrounded by a short brick wall.

Outside the courtyard was the city proper. When they were being dragged through the streets, Aramis had seen both houses and shops. It was a self-sustaining city, full of people. Women and children wandered the streets freely. All of the men, it seemed, were priests of Mordum who remained secluded inside the temple.

As he looked around, he noticed a group of priests coming towards them. He braced himself, ready to fight the moment they cut him loose. They passed by him, dragging a man in their midst. They tied the man to one of the poles and continued on toward the temple. Aramis was surprised the man was even breathing.

"The priests must have beaten him badly," Mel said.

Aramis could tell that as well. The man was covered in blood and bruises. "I wonder who he is, and why they brought him here?"

Mel shrugged. "There's no telling when it comes to the followers of Mordum."

Aramis tried to get his hands loose from the ropes again. He grunted in pain as they ripped his skin open. He gave up again and sagged against the pole, defeated. Mel was staring at him. "We're going to die here, aren't we?" he asked.

"Of course not," Mel answered. "Edria will aid us."

Some of the priests that brought the new prisoner returned. One of them was carrying a curved sword. They approached the battered man and began to question him.

"Where is he?" one of them asked.

The man groaned lowly. Aramis wasn't even sure the man was conscious. They began to punch the man and slam his head back against the wooden pole. He cried out weakly.

"What is wrong with you?" Aramis shouted. "Leave him alone!"

The priest carrying the sword glanced over at him momentarily but turned his attention back to the prisoner. They pointedly ignored his protests. After several minutes of continued abuse, the priest with the sword finally pushed the other priests out of the way. In one deft movement, he lifted the blade and hacked the man's arm off at the shoulder.

Blood went everywhere. The poor man didn't make a sound. The priest continued to cut the man's limbs off one at a time. His other arm, then each leg. Aramis vomited. He was no novice to battle and had seen his fair share of injuries, but this was careless murder.

The priest cut the robes that bound the man and his body fell onto the ground. The other priests gathered the limbs and carried them back to the temple. The remaining priest walked over and stood before him. Aramis could see the blood dripping from the priest's sword. He met the man's eyes, sickened.

The priest lifted his sword as if to strike him. Aramis closed his eyes and waited to die. His hands were suddenly free. He opened his eyes, confused. The priest grabbed him by the back of his shirt and forced him toward the temple.

Aramis was about to fight, but when he looked over at Mel, his friend subtly shook his head. He considered the fact that they were in the middle of a city controlled by Mordum and decided not to fight or try to run. The priest placed the tip of the sword against his back and led him through the courtyard and into the temple.

As soon as they entered the stone building, Aramis was assaulted by a horrid smell. He had smelled something similar once during a battle. A rotting corpse had been left on the field in the sun. He tried not to gag.

The priest guided him through a long hallway and into a room that Aramis would have thought was from a nightmare. Blood covered the floor and was splattered on the walls. He noticed the priest treading carefully behind him, careful not to slip in the mess.

Aramis considered running for a brief moment but decided it wasn't worth the risk. Where would he go? He was trapped in the stronghold of Mordum's followers. They exited the bloody room through one of several doors and entered a narrow hall. It would have been difficult for two men to walk beside each other in the small space. They entered another room with severed limbs laying on tables of various shapes and sizes.

He was beginning to realize just how morbid these people were. Exiting that room as well, the priest stopped outside another door.

"Wait here," the priest warned, his glare promising torture if he was disobeyed.

Aramis didn't answer but stood rubbing his sore and bloodied wrists. The priest knocked twice before pushing the door open and disappearing within. Glancing around the hall, Aramis saw the priests weren't much for decoration, except for the blood and body parts. The priest opened the door and motioned for Aramis to enter.

He hesitated for just a moment, unsure of what might greet him inside this room. He stepped in and was immediately taken by surprise. The walls were covered with beautifully woven tapestries of vibrant colors, the floors covered with thick, plush rugs. A massive bookcase covered the back wall of the room, overfilled with books. The priest gave him another look of warning and left the room.

Aramis couldn't believe the wealth displayed in the place. A large desk sat in front of the bookcase and he suddenly realized there was someone sitting at it. The room was well lit, which provided him a perfect view of the man.

The first thing he noticed about the man was his bald head. It seemed to gleam in the lamplight. He wore a black cuirass with the symbol of Mordum—the upside-down cross—in silver on the left side of the chest. He sported a long horseshoe mustache that reached a few inches off his chin. As the man looked up at him, Aramis felt the tattoo on his arm tingle. He resisted the urge to scratch it.

"I've been waiting for you," the man said. His voice was deep and baritone.

"That's news to me," Aramis answered dryly.

The right side of the man's face rose in a smile. He stood up from his desk and put his hands behind his back. "Allow me to introduce myself. My name is Ilias. Mordum told me you were coming." He pulled the sleeve of his left arm up to reveal the symbol of the god. It was similar to Aramis's own tattoo, but Ilias's had a sword behind the cross. "I am the Prophet of Mordum," Ilias said.

"Then you are responsible for my father's murder?" Aramis growled angrily.

Ilias frowned. "I'm afraid I don't know what you're talking about. Who is your father?"

Aramis didn't believe the man. "My father was the king of Oakvalor."

"You are *him*," Ilias said softly. "'And behold, He shall come from a royal bloodline.'"

"What are you talking about?" Aramis asked.

"You are the promised one of Mordum," Ilias answered. "Long ago, he walked the earth in a mortal body. He seeks to do so again and he has chosen you to make this happen." Ilias shook his head in disbelief. "You must feel honored."

Aramis laughed. "I don't believe in any divine

figure," he said. "And I certainly haven't been chosen for anything beyond my own choices."

"It doesn't matter whether you believe it or not," Ilias chided. "It is the truth. Truth is not dependent upon belief or faith, it simply *is*."

"Regardless, I will never aid a murderer. If you lead those who follow Mordum, then you are responsible for my father's murder."

"I assure you I don't know what you mean. Why would I have killed your father? For what purpose or to what gain would I do such a thing?"

"You tell me. Your assassin killed him. I saw it with my own eyes. And then he cursed me with this!" Aramis yelled, pointing at his tattoo.

Ilias regarded him silently for a long while before responding. "Was this assassin wearing anything that caught your eye? A pendant of some sort?"

"I don't remember."

"Hm. How did he curse you with that tattoo? Tell me exactly what happened."

Aramis related the events of that horrible night. He described how he saw the man scaling the castle walls, his attempt to protect his father, and the murder. As he finished the story, he found his anger had subsided and was replaced with sadness. *I miss him so much,* he thought.

"Have you seen this man since then?" Ilias asked.

Aramis nodded. "Twice. Once in the Viss Mountains. My friend Mel called him a—" he tried to remember the word—"templar?"

"When was the second time you saw him?"

"He's the one who brought us here as prisoners," Aramis answered.

Ilias's face became like stone. "I see. Tell me, what were you doing so far from Oakvalor if you don't serve Mordum? This is his city, after all."

"I was hunting down my father's killer." Aramis didn't bother to mention he was also trying to retrieve the blood from the shrine. "And the trail led me here. Mel and I got caught in some traps in the woods."

"This place is a highly guarded secret. Surely someone told you where this city was. Who was it?"

Aramis shook his head. "No one told me anything. I didn't even know a city was out here. We just followed the assassin."

"I don't believe you," Ilias said. "Though that matters little. Mordum told me you were coming and that you would be the one to ensure he walks the earth again. Whether this is by your own choice, or by Mordum's will, I know it will come to pass. However, I cannot allow you to leave the city. And I cannot allow your friend to live."

Aramis stepped toward him. Ilias smiled as he touched his tattoo and Aramis froze in place. It was a strange feeling not being able to control his own body. He struggled with everything he could muster to no avail.

"You see," Ilias said, "as the Prophet of Mordum, I am given authority over everyone who bears the mark. I can *make* you do anything I desire, even if it violates your conscience. Show me reverence."

Aramis felt the muscles in his legs work of their own accord, moving and bending until he was on his knees before Ilias.

"You will kill the priest of Edria with your own hands," Ilias said malevolently. "Repeat it to me."

Aramis fought desperately to keep his mouth shut, but he heard the words come out of his mouth anyway. "I will kill Melchiades." As soon as he uttered them, deep inside he knew that Ilias really was going to make him kill his friend.

● ∞ ● ∞ ●

An hour later, Aramis was led out into the courtyard of the temple. When he saw that Mel was there as well, guarded by several priests, he knew the situation did not bode well. Ilias was there also, seated beneath a small pavilion. The priest leading Aramis took him to the center of the large area, directly across from Mel. Many of the priests gathered around the area, forming a wall around Mel and himself with their bodies. After they had enclosed the entire area, Ilias stood up.

"Brothers! Listen well. We have in our midst one of Edria's own warriors. How does he dare enter our holy city? His fellows murder our faithful, trying to snuff us out. And then he enters this place trying to do the same! Yet I declare to you that it will not work. Mordum himself fights on our behalf!" A cheer rang out from the gathered priests.

"To prove our god is stronger than Edria, we will have her pawn fight one of our faithful!" Aramis watched Mel standing resolute, outwardly seeming unfazed by the entire thing. Aramis hoped that Mel wasn't freaking out on the inside like he was. "Priest of Edria, summon your blade!"

Mel crossed his arms in defiance. Judging by the look on Ilias's face, Aramis could guess he wasn't pleased.

"Suit yourself," Ilias said. "You'll summon it if you want to live. Let the faithful one of Mordum step forth!" Aramis felt his muscles disobey his mind as he walked forward and lift his hand in salute to the Prophet.

Mel's arms uncrossed and slowly came to rest at his sides. He turned his head curiously, wondering what was happening.

"Aramis, the chosen one of Mordum, has honored our god by pledging to kill this vile intruder!" Another cheer rang out. "Choose your weapon!"

Aramis didn't want to choose a weapon. And he certainly didn't want to fight Mel. Yet his body was under the control of Ilias, and he could only watch helplessly. He walked over to one of the priests and took their sword, then returned to the center.

"Kill him!" Ilias shouted.

Aramis walked closer to Mel, swinging the sword in front of him in small 'X' shapes. He could feel his muscles loosening from the effort. He tried to shake his head or say something, to do anything that would warn his friend.

"I won't fight you," Mel said to him as he got closer. Aramis tilted his head to each side until it cracked, then did the same with his back. He lunged forward, stabbing towards Mel's stomach. His friend easily slapped the blade away with his hand as he leaped out of the way. "I'm not going to fight you," he said again, the confusion evident in his voice.

Aramis didn't bother trying to respond. He couldn't do anything to thwart Ilias's hold over him. He turned to the left and swung again, narrowly missing Mel's right arm. Ilias must have been getting impatient with Mel, for Aramis's attacks became faster and more furious.

Mel continued to dodge and evade the attacks, but Aramis could tell it was getting harder for him not to engage. Aramis scored a strike to his leg, opening a large gash in Mel's flesh. Mel grunted in pain and finally summoned his sword. Aramis felt fear rise within him. What if Ilias had his way and he killed Mel? Or if Mel, in self-defense, had to kill him? He didn't see any good outcome to their situation.

"I don't know what you are doing," Mel panted, "but I will not fight you. I will die if need be to ensure you live."

If he had control of his body, he likely would have teared up at Mel's loyalty. *I'm sorry*, he thought, wishing Mel could hear him. And then he rushed his friend, swinging the sword in a powerful arc. Mel brought his own blade up and blocked the blow, then pushed his arm out wide, throwing Aramis's sword from his grasp.

Aramis quickly retrieved the blade, thankful that Mel didn't take the advantage and try to strike him. Many men could be loyal, but when it came to life and death, loyalty usually went out the window. He had known Mel long enough to know that he was more honorable than anyone he had met, but their friendship had never been tested like this.

Trust Melchiades, for he will not lead you astray. The words of the old blind woman echoed in his mind. Aramis did trust him. He trusted Mel like a brother. So it came as a surprise when Mel attacked him. Aramis staggered back, deflecting the attack. Mel didn't let up and knocked Aramis to the ground. He put the point of his sword to Aramis's throat.

"Your champion has been defeated," Mel said to Ilias.

Ilias laughed. "You fool, this isn't a duel. This is a fight to the death."

Mel removed the blade from Aramis's neck. "I won't kill him," he said.

"You *can't* kill him," Ilias replied.

Before Mel could move, Aramis forced himself up and threw himself against Mel's blade. It punctured the skin of his neck and Aramis could feel the blade sever his windpipe. He coughed and choked as blood filled his airway. He slumped back onto the ground and saw the horror on Mel's face.

I'm dying! His mind screamed at him. His vision began to fade as he struggled to breathe. He finally had control of his body, but there was nothing he could do to save himself. He closed his eyes as he felt death sweep over him.

And then he opened them. He could breathe again. He reached up to his neck and felt nothing but smooth skin. "What—" he was about to say 'happened' before he felt the control of his body slip out of his grasp. He stood back up and retrieved the sword that had fallen out of his hand. Mel was staring at him incredulously.

"Mordum is God of the Dead," Ilias stated loudly, "and therefore Aramis cannot die unless I allow it. Now kill that Edrian scum!"

Aramis launched himself at Mel, trying to strike him in the chest. For some reason, Mel had yet to summon his armor. They continued back and forth, trading blows with one another and both receiving cuts and scrapes. Aramis lifted his sword up high to bring it down for a killing stroke when Mel's blade came at him suddenly, slicing the tattooed skin of his left arm.

He felt Ilias's hold break immediately. He flung the sword down and staggered away from Mel, raising his hands in surrender. "It's me!" he yelled. "It's me! Ilias was controlling me! I'm sorry for attacking you!"

Mel summoned his armor, the air shimmering with mist as it formed. "I figured something was going on when you cut my leg," he said. "I don't see any other option than to fight our way out." Aramis nodded and picked his sword back up.

"Kill the priest and take Aramis captive!" Ilias commanded. The wall of priests began to close in around them. Aramis surrendered himself to the fact that although he didn't kill Mel, these priests certainly would. They were seriously outnumbered. Aramis readied himself.

A horn sounded in the distance. The encroaching priests hesitated, glancing around uncertainly. A second horn sounded, this one closer and louder than the first.

"What's that?" Aramis asked, casting a brief glance

at Mel.

"I'm not sure, but it sounds like Orcish war horns."

A priest came running from the city area, shouting for the Prophet. He reached Ilias, panting and out of breath. "They're coming," he said.

"Who is coming?" Ilias demanded.

"Orcs!"

Ilias turned to look at Mel and Aramis, seeming to struggle internally with some decision. "Forget the priest," he commanded. "Defend the city! An army of orcs approaches!"

The priests quickly scattered, heading toward the walls that protected the city's borders. Ilias continued to stare at Aramis.

"We've got to get out of here," Mel said.

"We can't leave without the blood," Aramis replied.

"Any ideas where it might be? We don't have much time."

"I'm sure the priests will be busy with the orcs for a while," Aramis said, turning toward the temple. "It has to be in there."

"I'm not worried about the orcs," Mel said. "I took a chance at slicing your tattoo, but from what I saw a moment ago, it's not going to be long before your skin heals itself and Ilias takes control of you again. We need to be long gone before that happens."

"Wait, you didn't know for sure it would work?"

"Of course not. How could I?"

Aramis shrugged. They ran towards the temple and entered to find the halls empty. Apparently, all of the priests were present for the fight. They began searching through every room they encountered. Many of them seemed to be lodgings for the priests.

"In here!" Mel called out. Aramis left the room he was searching and ran to where Mel was. It was the room with the severed body parts on the tables. On one of them was the wineskin they had used to collect the blood from the shrine.

Aramis grabbed it and they ran back into the hall, trying to navigate their way back out of the building. "What are they doing in that room?" Aramis asked. "It looks like something out of a nightmare."

"There's no telling with Mordum," Mel answered.

They escaped the building and ended up back in the courtyard. Ilias was nowhere to be found. They made their way toward the city area. The sounds of battle could be heard in every direction. Women were screaming and children were running through the streets, trying to find somewhere to hide.

They turned a corner and almost ran into a large orc. The orc cut down a priest and turned to face them. Aramis brought his sword up and was about to charge the creature when Mel stopped him. The orc nodded at Mel.

"I see you are still following your god," the orc said.

"And I see you are out for revenge for your kin," Mel answered.

The orc growled. "These priests will feel the fury of my anger for their betrayal!"

"I pray that you will get what you seek, my friend. Can you point us to the way out?"

"I can show you the way out, but this one must stay with me," the orc said, pointing to Aramis. "He wears their brand on his arm."

"He's not a follower," Mel said. "He was cursed by the Templar who betrayed you on the mountain. He's with me."

Aramis thought the orc was going to refuse to let him leave, but then he bowed his head. "I trust your judgment. Follow the road that leads to the east. It will take you out of the city. Fight well, my friend."

"Thank you," Mel said. They turned to leave, only to

find the templar from the mountain blocking their way.

"Out of the way!" the orc roared. "He's mine!"

Aramis and Mel both stepped aside quickly as the massive creature charged the priest. As they crashed into each other, Aramis and Mel took advantage of the distraction and quickly ran past them, continuing down the road.

"I hope the orc doesn't kill the priest," Aramis said between breaths. "I want to be the one to kill that murderer."

"He won't," Mel replied. "The templar will crush him, so we don't have much time. We need to get as far as we can before he catches up to us."

Aramis looked down at his arm as he felt the tattoo on his skin begin to itch. The skin was healed.

"Kings will tremble in fear and cities will crumble."

—The Prophet of Mordum

CHAPTER 19

Aramis and Mel ran along the worn path, weaving among the trees. Aramis kept one hand clutched against the wineskin of blood at his waist to ensure it didn't come loose.

"We've got to hurry," Mel huffed.

"I'm moving as fast as I can," Aramis replied. His lungs and his legs were burning. The fact they hadn't eaten anything wasn't helping either. He could feel the dry blood from his wrists on his palms and fingers. "I'm afraid we aren't going to make it," he said. "It's too far."

"We have to try," Mel answered.

Aramis thought he could faintly hear hoof beats behind them. "They've noticed our escape. We can't outrun horses. We've got to find some place to hide."

"I agree, my Prince. But I don't see anywhere worthy of being called a hiding spot here in the trees."

Aramis knew Mel was right. It didn't look good for them. The path suddenly veered right and led them out of the trees and onto the main road. He cursed their luck and stopped running. Mel stopped beside him. Aramis looked back and could see a lone horseman riding his way through the trees.

"It took us over a week to get here by carriage and horse, Mel. I don't see a way out of this."

"Not for both of us," Mel answered.

Aramis looked to him, confused. "What do you mean?"

The air rippled as Mel summoned his sword. "We both can't get away. One of us will need to be a diversion."

"Mel, you said yourself that very few have defeated a templar. Don't put your life at risk on account of me."

"Once they catch us, they'll kill me anyway. If I can give you time to get away, then you at least have a chance of getting the blood to the Prophet. We cannot allow the blood to fall back into their hands. Go, Aramis."

"I'm not leaving you," Aramis said defiantly.

"You have to. There is more at stake here than one man's life. You have to go. Use the mark to aid you. I know I've been telling you to fight the sway of Mordum, but the power of his curse may offer some help. Go."

Aramis didn't move.

"Go!" Mel screamed. The horseman reached the road. Aramis looked from Mel to the templar. He didn't feel right about leaving his friend behind. In the army, they taught that a soldier should never be left behind. Aramis knew what Mel said was true, however. If Mordum walked the earth as a man, Hell would come with him. There *was* more at stake than one man's life, no matter if it was his friend or not.

"Go!" Mel screamed again.

Aramis grit his teeth in anger. There was no other option. He turned and fled.

● ∞ ● ∞ ●

Mel watched over his shoulder as Aramis sprinted off. He nodded in grim satisfaction. "Goodbye, my friend." He turned to face the templar, who had dismounted and was approaching deliberately.

"He won't get far," the templar said. "After I destroy you, he will be next. You cannot stop Mordum." The templar pulled his hood back and held his hand out, summoning his own blade. The air hissed as the black blade came into existence.

Mel got into his battle stance, holding his sword up before him. He watched the templar carefully. Though he had never fought one of Mordum's Knights before, he had learned enough from the Prophet's tales to know they could be very powerful.

The templar leaped forward suddenly. He was much quicker than Mel expected, but he was able to parry the attack. He launched into his own attack, twisting his blade about and striking the templar's armor twice, resulting in two jagged lines on the otherwise flawless armor.

The templar laughed. Lightning flickered along his blade and he struck Mel's shoulder. It bounced off the plate harmlessly, but the shock made Mel flinch involuntarily. They exchanged several blows, weighing each other's weaknesses. Mel knew immediately that he was outmatched. He had to injure the templar or hold him off long enough for Aramis to get a decent head start. He knew it wasn't likely.

● ∞ ● ∞ ●

Aramis ran as fast as he could, which wasn't very fast. He was exhausted, hungry, and sore. He looked back several times, but he couldn't tell what was happening. Why did Mel have to be so blasted righteous? Giving his life so Aramis could *try* to escape. It wasn't even a guarantee. He fought back the tears as he thought of the violent end Mel would likely meet at the templar's hands.

He slipped on a rock and twisted his ankle, tumbling down onto the ground. He grunted in pain. He'd had worse injuries before, but if he couldn't walk on it, he certainly wouldn't get far before the templar reached him. He got up and took a few steps, gritting his teeth in agony. His ankle burned like fire.

Use the mark.

Mel's words echoed in his mind. Aramis looked at the tattoo, disgusted by it. The mark of the god responsible for everything that had gone wrong in his life the last few weeks might be his only chance at survival. The irony wasn't lost on him.

Mel said before that the mark had all kinds of effects on people. He was wary of trying to use it. He could just as likely go insane as he could gain power that others could only dream of. The most obvious problem was that he didn't even know how to use the tattoo. Did he just need to touch it? Or did he will it to work?

"I've got to try something," he said to himself. He closed his eyes and focused on the tattoo. He pictured it in his mind and willed it to let him walk without pain. He opened his eyes and took a step. His ankle screamed in rebellion and he almost fell again. He kept his weight off of it as he tried everything he could think of to try and activate the tattoo. Finally, he touched it with his finger. He felt … *something* … run along his arm.

It was a strong tingling feeling that threatened numbness, like the time he was almost struck by lightning on the castle walls. The air had thrummed with electricity. It was almost the same.

Almost.

There was something different about this feeling.

With the lightning, there had been the fear of dying. Not with this. This felt good. *Really* good. It called his name, begging to be released. So he released it. Power flowed through his body, overwhelming him. His body convulsed violently before he lost his sight.

There was nothing but darkness.

● ∞ ● ∞ ●

Mel was struggling just to defend himself. He parried the attacks as fast as he could, but he was getting sluggish. It must have been obvious, for the templar began attacking faster. He prayed to Edria for strength, but none came. There was nothing but a disturbing silence. And then the realization struck him. Edria had abandoned him. That knowledge was worse than the fact that he knew he would not survive this battle.

If it was his time to die, then so be it. But he couldn't bear the thought that his goddess had forsaken him. Was it because of Aramis? Was it because he had decided in his heart not to obey the Prophet about leaving the prince to die? If so, he didn't understand. All life was sacred. How could Edria forsake him for refusing to let an innocent man die?

He tried to push the thoughts from his mind. The templar thrust at him. Mel barely deflected the blow and was surprised when the templar followed through with a vicious kick to his knee. His leg buckled, but thankfully he didn't go down. He brought his blade up and to the left, going for an attack in the opening the templar left. Too late, Mel realized it was a ruse. The templar's blade plunged into his stomach, slicing through his armor, flesh, and bone before ripping out through his back.

He gasped in shock. His own sword slipped from his hand and fell to the ground at his feet. The templar jerked the blade forward roughly, forcing Mel to stagger backward. He clutched his stomach as the templar withdrew his sword from his body. Black dots ringed the outside of his vision. Blood poured freely over his hands. Oddly, he thought to himself that he needed to sit down. But the thought didn't make any sense, because he knew he was battling for his life.

Suddenly he was on his back staring up into the sky. It was so *blue*. He'd never noticed before how blue it really was. Then he saw the templar looking down at him with a wicked grin.

"Now your friend dies," he said.

And then he no longer saw the man. He heard the sound of a horse galloping away. Something in his mind told him that Aramis was going to die, but for some reason, he didn't care. He wanted to care, but he just … couldn't.

He was bleeding to death. He couldn't see anything now, but he was sure he had his eyes open. As he exhaled for the last time, he thought he heard the sound of a merchant's cart.

And then he died.

● ∞ ● ∞ ●

Release me.

Aramis looked to where he heard a voice calling faintly. It was coming from the other side of a large wooden door. As he walked toward the door, he realized he was back home at the castle. The door was to his father's room. He put his hand on the handle, then hesitated. What would it be like to walk back into that room?

He gritted his teeth as tears stung his eyes and opened the door. His father stood there, gazing out the window. Aramis stopped mid-step in confusion.

"My son," his father's voice greeted him.

"Father?"

"You sound surprised," his father said without turning around.

"I … I saw you die," Aramis said softly.

"You must have dreamed it," his father replied.

Death cannot contain me.

"What?"

"I said you must have dreamed it."

"What did you say after that?" Aramis asked.

"I didn't say anything, son. What's going on with you? Are you feeling well?"

Aramis felt confused. He looked around the room for anything that seemed out of the ordinary. Everything seemed normal. Had he really dreamed everything? Was his father still alive? He hoped it was true.

"Father, what happened last night?" he asked.

"What do you mean?"

"What happened last night? Do you remember?"

"Of course I remember. Are you drunk, boy? We were out riding after our hunt."

Aramis stared at the man who seemed to be his father. "We didn't go riding, or on a hunt," he replied. "We had a feast."

His father didn't answer. Aramis stepped closer and laid his hand on his father's shoulder. A sharp coldness ran up his arm and he cried out in surprise. His father turned around, only it wasn't his father. The man's face was pale and thin.

"Mordum!" Aramis exclaimed, stepping back from the man.

Release me.

"I am your father."

"No!" he yelled. "You cannot fool me with your tricks!"

"I have given you a new life," Mordum said. "I have taken away the sting of death. And now I will give you power among men. They will see your deeds and know your power comes from *me*. Now go."

Aramis backed away and reached to his belt for his sword. The scabbard was empty.

"Go. Go forth and *release me!*"

Aramis turned to flee and saw that he was on the road. He looked around frantically, fearing Mordum was there as well. He was alone. In the distance, he could see someone coming. He couldn't be sure, but he thought he could also see a horse. The templar.

He prepared himself for the pain as he tried to start walking. There was no pain. He rolled his foot around and put his full weight on his hurt foot.

Nothing.

He didn't have time to contemplate the sudden change. He started running, trying to gain ground on the approaching horseman. He knew it was foolish to think he could outrun a horse, but what other options did he have?

He ran as fast as he could. And that's when he noticed it. Everything was flying past him speedily. Aramis looked over his shoulder and didn't even see the rider. He slowed to a jog. He'd only run for a few minutes, but it seemed like he had covered a lot of distance.

I will give you power among men.

Aramis wondered if that was a good thing. If it gave him the ability to escape and take the blood to the Prophet, then perhaps there might be some good in wielding Mordum's powers. He increased his speed and watched as the scenery flew by. At this rate, he'd make it back in half the time.

● ∞ ● ∞ ●

After three days, Aramis finally reached the city. He

was drenched in sweat and covered in dirt. None of that mattered to him. He had the blood from the shrine and the Prophet would now give him the support he would need to begin clearing his name. He would not let Mel's sacrifice be in vain. He entered the church's compound and was greeted by a small group of priests.

"I need to see the Prophet," he informed them.

One of the priests held his hand up as if to block him. "The Prophet speaks with the people of the city during the weekly service. He's currently unavailable."

"That's great," Aramis said impatiently. "I'm not here for that. He sent me on a mission with Melchiades."

"A mission?" The priest looked at his cohorts. "I'm not aware of any mission. What exactly did he send you off to do?"

Aramis pulled the wineskin from his belt. "To retrieve this blood from the shrine of Mordum."

All of the priests began talking at once. The one who had spoken commanded silence from them. "My apologies," the priest said. "I'll take you to him immediately. Follow me." The man led Aramis into the building, the other priests falling in behind them. He recognized the hallway to the Prophet's office as soon as they turned down it.

"Wait here," the priest said before entering into the room. He returned and held the door open for Aramis to enter.

The Prophet was standing by the map table, looking expectantly at him. "You've brought the blood?" he asked. There was an excitement to his tone that wasn't lost on Aramis.

"I have," he answered.

"This is good news. Where is Melchiades?"

"He …" words failed him. He swallowed hard and tried to speak again, but nothing came out. Finally, he simply shook his head.

"I see," the Prophet said somberly. "His sacrifice will not be forgotten. Melchiades was a great man, ardent in his faith. He will be greatly missed."

Aramis could only nod in agreement.

"Where is the blood?"

Aramis held the wineskin out to him. The Prophet gingerly accepted it and set it on his desk.

"I'm grateful that you managed to retrieve the blood, and I know it cost you a lot to do so."

"I trust you will give me your support in trying to clear my name?" Aramis asked.

The Prophet stood tall and looked Aramis in the eyes. "I'm sorry, but I cannot do that. You wear the mark of Mordum openly on your skin. The fact that you returned with the blood so easily tells me that you truly are a servant of Mordum. Escort Aramis to the dungeon." He motioned to the other priests. They obeyed quickly and grabbed Aramis by his arms.

"What are you doing?" Aramis demanded. "You said if I got you that blood you would help me!"

"About that," the Prophet said, "I lied. Take him now."

Aramis struggled to get free, but the priests dragged him out by force. They pulled him through the church's halls and finally down the stairs that led to the dungeon. He continued to struggle against them, but it was no use. He was outmatched. They tossed him into one of the cells and locked the door. He shook the bars of the gate.

"You can't do this!" he screamed. "You can't do this to me!"

No one was listening.

"Order is not pressure which is imposed on society from without, but an equilibrium which is set up from within."

—General Garrick

CHAPTER 20

Garrick waited until his wife was asleep to move. He gently kissed her forehead before rolling off the bed. They had left a window cracked and a cool breeze wafted through the opening. He grabbed a robe from the closet and covered his nakedness.

Making his way to the study, the few guards he passed lowered their heads in reverence to him. He had worked hard and given much to help the people of Talvaard. Thanks to his men—who had bravely fought against the tyranny of the others—and to Aramis, tomorrow he would be king. The details of the coronation were being planned by the court chamberlain, with a little help from his wife.

He hoped she would get pregnant soon. Now that the kingdom was reunited, life would return to normal and he could focus on the good of the people and raising a family. He smiled as he imagined what his children might look like. His sons would be strong like him, his daughters beautiful like his wife. All that he had worked for was certainly worth it.

Garrick entered the study to find that the servants had already prepared it for him. A desk made of cedar sat to the left. To the right, numerous bookstands lined the enormous room with books on every subject imaginable. He was thankful that the kings before him had been learned men, choosing to be educated not only in war. He walked among the stands, reading some of the titles on the books.

A History of Talvaard.
The Book of Faith.
The Sayings of Kings.
The Persecution of Mages.

He decided suddenly that he would make plans to read every book in the study. It might take him the rest of his life, but it would be a great accomplishment. He walked to the table and sat down. Two silver bowls, one on each side of the desk, were filled with glow stones. They glowed a faint bluish color. Often cheaper to use than candles or lanterns, the stones were usually found in the same mines as gold. Although stones had been found in almost every color, the predominant hue found was blue. No one was quite sure why the rocks gave off the light, but many offered varying conjectures.

A decently sized stack of papers had been placed on the desk, all needing to be signed. Grabbing one of the quills on the desk, he dipped it into an inkwell and was about to sign the first paper when he paused. There was no telling what the documents might contain, so he began reading. He found many of them disagreeable and placed them to the side. The others he signed and placed in a separate pile, then he went back to the others. He crossed out lines he didn't agree with and added things he thought should be included.

By the time he was finished, several hours had passed. His eyes were burning from reading so long, but otherwise, he wasn't very tired. He knew it was well after midnight. Perhaps it was his excitement over the coronation, but he simply couldn't sleep. He grabbed the two piles of papers and left the study. A young man in the robes of a monk was standing outside the door.

"Good evening, Your Majesty," the monk greeted.

"I've not been crowned king yet," Garrick replied. "But I appreciate the sentiment."

The monk smiled and bowed his head. "My apologies. Is there anything I can do to serve you tonight?"

Garrick held out the papers. "These have been signed and are ready to be issued. These ones here need to be re-written and brought back to me."

"Re-written, Your Maj—" the monk paused momentarily before correcting himself, "My Lord?"

"Yes. I don't like what they propose, so I've made changes and want them fixed. I will not sign anything until I have read it and agree with it."

"That is wise, my Lord. I will deliver them and pass along your message." The monk took the papers and disappeared down the hall.

Garrick rubbed the back of his neck. Staring down at those papers so long had put a crick in it. He wandered along the hallways, pausing to admire the many statues and tapestries that decorated the palace. Eventually, he entered the throne room where he would listen to petitions from the people and the nobles. He surveyed the design etched in the floor and wondered if it signified anything.

The vaulted ceiling rose sixty feet above him. Support pillars were spaced every ten feet, outlining the main walkway through the chamber. Two giant alabaster statues of winged men standing at attention flanked either side of a door located in the middle of the far wall. Portraits of regal men, the kings of the past, were spaced along the entire chamber. Garrick spent time staring at each one. He wondered what each man's character had been like. He was only slightly familiar with the reign of the older kings. Perhaps he would read some books that recorded the events of their reign.

He made his way to the door flanked by the statues and entered it. He found a hallway large enough for two carriages to comfortably pass through. There were a couple of doors but they were all locked. He made a note to investigate the hall when he had the keys to the doors. He turned around and went back into the throne room.

The events of the day were starting to wear him down. He returned to his room to find his wife still sleeping. He returned the robe and climbed back into bed, kissing his wife on the forehead again before laying on his back. He closed his eyes.

It seemed as if he had just drifted off when he heard something. Garrick's eyes snapped open and he sat straight up in the bed. He looked to his wife. She was still sleeping. Had he really just fallen asleep, or had it been several hours? He looked around the room, trying to figure out what had woken him. Someone knocked at his bedroom door.

In his tiredness, he forgot he was naked and opened the door. The hallway lights had been dimmed for the night. He was greeted by a guard and one of his captains. "My King," the Captain bowed. "I hate to wake you, but if it wasn't urgent you know I wouldn't."

"Of course. What is wrong?"

The Captain glanced at the guard, then back to Garrick. "Perhaps you'd like to get dressed first?"

Garrick looked down at himself. "Excuse me," he said. He shut the door, retrieved his robe, and then stepped out into the hallway. "Report Styrmir."

Styrmir pulled a rolled parchment from his waist and read it to Garrick. "The northern border was attacked and three cities have been destroyed. Two of them were smaller villages, but one was a decently fortified city. Hundreds are feared dead. Most of those who escaped made it to the closest city, a few of them managed to get here to report it."

Garrick listened intently. "Who is behind the attack? If someone is trying to rebel against my rule, I will banish them from Talvaard."

Styrmir shook his head. "No, it wasn't any of the generals. The report says it was elves."

"Elves?" Garrick was dumbfounded. "From the Deadlands?"

Styrmir nodded grimly. "Yes. I didn't believe it at first, but when more than one of the survivors had the same story, I requested a report from Captain Ghottard in the north." He held the parchment up. "This is the official report. According to best guesses, it sounds like the elves had a large force, possibly in the thousands."

"Has Captain Ghottard mounted an offensive?"

"No, sir. He wants to, but he doesn't have enough men. He seems confident that he can hold the city if they attack, though he is requesting reinforcements."

"The elves are still in the area?" Garrick asked, still trying to wrap his mind around it.

"They are. They've set up camp a few miles from Ghottard's city."

"How many men does he have available right now?"

"Five hundred, maybe. I've ordered two battalions of three hundred each to march immediately. Obviously, it will take them a few days to get there. Is this sufficient, or should I send more?"

Garrick folded his arms across his chest. After giving it some thought he said, "That should be sufficient. The elves are barbarians. They don't have the defenses or weapons we do. I don't know how they took a fortified city, but they won't be doing it again. Thank you for bringing this information to me. It is troubling indeed."

"I knew that you'd want to be informed immediately. We finally have peace in the kingdom. We don't need it shattering now."

"I agree," Garrick said. "Thank you again." Styrmir bowed and left. The soldier guarding his door saluted Garrick with a hand to his chest. Garrick returned the salute and went back into his bedroom. He was deeply troubled. Why would elves be attacking his cities? He noticed his wife was sitting up in bed.

"What's wrong?" she asked sleepily. "Why aren't you in bed?"

"Nothing is wrong, my love. Styrmir brought some important news. He's handling it, but he wanted to inform me."

"Okay," she said. "Come back to bed then."

"I will in a moment. First I must pray. Go back to sleep, my beauty. I'll be back shortly." She laid back down among the pillows and rolled over. He left the room and made his way back to the study. The monk who was there before must have retired for he wasn't to be found. Garrick entered the chamber and closed the door behind him. There didn't appear to be a locking mechanism, but he didn't expect many people to be up so late.

He sat at the desk and pulled the left sleeve of his arm up. The flesh was smooth and tan. He scratched at the flesh about an inch above his wrist until a small piece of skin came up. He pinched the skin and pulled slowly but firmly. As the skin was removed, a dark tattoo began to take shape. Garrick pulled a rectangular piece of skin off, roughly five inches long by two inches wide. He set it on the desk and looked it over.

It wasn't skin at all, but a fabric type of material. It had been dyed to match his skin color and he held it in place using an adhesive liquid. It was a clever design he had commissioned a few years ago. Placing his index and middle finger on the tattoo, he closed his eyes.

"Mordum, hear my prayer …"

THE END OF BOOK TWO

ABOUT THE AUTHOR

Richard Fierce lives in Georgia with his wife and three step-daughters. He is the author of seven novels including Dragonsphere. Feel free to contact the author.

Email: <u>Richard.Fierce@yahoo.com</u>